David W. Allen

Genealogy

Biographical Sketches of the Descendants of Thomas and Anthony

Thacher

David W. Allen

Genealogy
Biographical Sketches of the Descendants of Thomas and Anthony Thacher

ISBN/EAN: 9783337098575

Printed in Europe, USA, Canada, Australia, Japan

Cover: Foto ©Raphael Reischuk / pixelio.de

More available books at **www.hansebooks.com**

GENEALOGY,

AND

Biographical Sketches,

OF THE

DESCENDANTS OF

THOMAS AND ANTHONY THACHER,

From their Settlement in New England,

JUNE 4th, 1635.

INDEPENDENT PRINTING HOUSE,
VINELAND, N. J.
1872.

THACHER COAT OF ARMS.

DESCRIPTION.—GULES, a cross moline *argent*, on a chief *d'or* three grasshoppers proper. Crest, a grasshopper proper.

PREFACE.

In offering this little record of the Genealogy of the **THACHER** family, we are aware of its incompleteness. Nearly two hundred and fifty years have elapsed since Anthony and Thomas Thacher landed in New England, and the family has become so numerous and so scattered that it would be very nearly impossible to make a complete record of them.

In compiling this little volume, we have been greatly assisted by a pamphlet published in July, 1834, by Dr. James Thacher, of Plymouth, Mass., entitled "Biographical Sketches of the Thacher family from their First Settlement in New England," which we have incorporated, with such changes and additions as subsequent records demanded. We are also largely indebted to M. W. Graves, Esq, of Hartford, Conn., and his sister, Julia A. Graves, for records obtained by them in the State Historical and Genealogical Rooms at Hartford, and to George Winslow Thacher, of New York, for very many important records.

This work was commenced by Mrs. Caroline Thatcher Cobb, of Saratoga Springs, N. Y., by whom very many of the later records were procured, and Miss Lucy E. Thacher (late Mrs. Allen) and we assume the publication of these records as a labor of love and respect for her memory. We should have been glad to have made them still more complete, but time and opportunity forbade. We return our thanks to the numerous members of the family who have so kindly furnished material for the book, and hope some future historian may be still more successful in preserving the records of this family, who have filled, by no means an unimportant part, in the annals of New England history.

D. W. ALLEN.

VINELAND, N J., June 1, 1872.

BIOGRAPHICAL SKETCHES

OF THE

THACHER FAMILY,

FROM THEIR

FIRST SETTLEMENT IN NEW ENGLAND.

———•———

"It has been the anxious desire of all nations, in all ages of the world, that family genealogies, from their original foundations, should be correctly recorded and transmitted to future generations; and posterity love to trace back their progenitors, in an uninterrupted line, to the earliest periods. The descendants of the puritan fathers of New England have a peculiar interest in the character and transactions of their ancestors, and they are happily furnished with ample data for the purpose of tracing the course of the founders of an empire. When the Saxons came over and settled in England, the British sirnames were immerged, and no records of the original inhabitants, by their own sirnames, were to be found on the page of history; but in our favored country by far the largest proportion of our sirnames are those which were precious to our puritan fathers, and ever will be to their grateful posterity. The spreading branches of the genealogical tree, from the stock of the pilgrims, will ever command admiration and respect; and, among these, the name of Thacher is not the least deserving of a grateful and perpetual remembrance. Whether the Thacher family were ever entitled to the distinction of ancient and honorable, the writer has not been ambitious to ascertain.

"The first of the name of which we have obtained any account, is the ' REV. PETER THACHER,* a distinguished Minister of the Gospel, who resided in Sarum, in England, in the seventeenth century. He was a man of talents, and possessed a liberal and independent mind: he dissented from the established church, and being in consequence harassed by the spiritual courts, he resolved to turn his back on royal and ecclesiastical folly and persecution, and emigrate to New England, for the enjoyment of religious freedom; but the death of his wife altered his determination. There is now a letter extant, which he wrote to the Bishop of the Diocese, begging that he might be excused from reading certain directions of the vicar-general, which, he said, were against his conscience; and would tend to disturb the order of worship. In his address, he says, 'I never neglected the order aforesaid out of contempt of ecclesiastical discipline and jurisdiction, as has been affirmed, &c. This may, perhaps, account for the puritanical zeal with which so many of the family have opposed the prelatic power, and may be one, among other causes, of the strong attachment of the descendants to good New England principles.' "

The following letter to the Dean of Salisbury, England, from H. Hatcher, the historian of Salisbury, we find in the Mass. His. Col., and seems to be in reply to a letter of inquiry addressed to the Dean by Mr. Savage, the author of "Savage's

* We find t his name spelled *Thacher* and *Thatcher* by different members of the family. The proper spelling of the name is not a matter of conjecture or a probability, but a matter of absolute certainty. The original autograph of Rev. Peter, of St. Edmunds, at least two of which are preserved in this country, and which still appear on the records of St. Edmunds, show that he spelled the name Thacher. The signature of his brother Anthony—which also appears on the same records—is spelled *Thacher*; and the autographs of several of their descendants, viz.: Rev. Thomas, of Old South, Rev. Peter, of Milton, Rev. Ralph, of Martha's Vineyard, Hon. John, of Yarmouth, and others, are still preserved and spelled the same way. Hon Stephen Thacher, of Biekland, Maine, who died in 1859, aged 83, and Hon Geo. Thacher, Judge of the Supreme Court of Massachusetts, both of whom took a deep interest in the history of the family, both spelled it so. The name *Thatcher* seems to have been adopted within the past one hundred years, and many of the later families spell it thus, but we do not feel at liberty to publish these records with that spelling, when so large a majority spell it Thacher, but shall endeavor, in cases of families who spell it *Thatcher*, to spell it as they do, believing that each one has a right to spell his or her name as they choose.

Gen. Dictionary," concerning several families whose genealogy
he wished to trace. We quote in part as follows:

SALISBURY, Nov. 19, 1842.

To the Very Reverend the Dean of Salisbury:
DEAR SIR—I send you these few scattering notices which I have
collected, relative to the persons mentioned in Mr. Savage's letter.
They are not as full as I could have wished; but they are quite as
much so as might be expected from the distance of time and the dis-
turbed state of the country at the commencement of the civil war.

As the Rev. Peter Thacher filled a public station for some years,
the information relating to him is much more abundant and distinct
than that preserved by the others. I do not believe him to have
been a native of Salisbury, though the name of Thacher twice occurs
in the register of St. Edmunds towards the close of the 16th century.
He was appointed minister of St. Edmunds in 1622, and the circumstances connected with his appointment are subjoined as they are
recorded in the Minute Book of the Vestry.

I ought to premise, that the right of patronage to the living of St.
Edmunds was then a matter of dispute between the bishop and certain inhabitants of the parish, who laid claim to it in consequence of
the transfer of the college, and the rights and property belonging to
it to William St. Bache at the dissolution.

The mode in which the living was filled for some years, is not
quite clear; but the immediate predecessor of Thacher was Hugh
Williams, who was presented by Bishop Cotton in 1606, and resigned
in 1620 or 22, apparently in consequence of a disagreement with the
leaders of the parish, who were Puritans. The cause was evidently
a diversity of religious opinion.

The writer proceeds to give the records of the Vestry which called
Mr. Thacher, which we cannot quote, and says: "From this account
it is evident that Mr. Thacher was brought in by the Puritan or Pres-
byterian party in the Vestry.

The word *come*, which is twice used, I consider as proof that he
was not previously a resident in the city.

His institution as Rector of St. Edmunds is recorded in the Bishop's
Book under the date of 1622.

The Bishop is mentioned as patron. This was Bishop Davenant,
who favored the Puritans and doubtless accepted the recommenda-
tion of the Vestry.

While Mr. Thacher was minister, the following notices occur relative to him and his family:

1623, Nov. —. Baptized dau. of Mr. Peter Thacher, parson of this
parish.

1625, Jan. 29. Baptized Elizabth, dau. of Mr. P. Thacher, minister
of this parish.

1627-8, Jan. 29. John, son to Mr. Peter Thacher, minister of this
parish.

1636-7, Jan. 1 Samuel, son of Mr. Peter Thacher.

1638. Paul, son of Mr. P. Thacher.

1640, Aug. —. Barnabas, son of Mr. P. Thacher.

In 1631 and '33 we find Anthony Thacher, probably his brother,
mentioned as curate In 1634, April 27, occurs this entry relative to
a son of Anthony Thacher: "Benjamin, son of Anthony and Mary

Thacher, born on Sunday, the 13th day, between the hours of one and two in the morning, and baptized the 27th of the same month. The name of Anthony Thacher appears again as curate in 1634." The writer gave an account of licenses granted by the parson, one beginning as follows: "I, Peter Thacher, Parson of the Parish Church of St. Edmunds, within the city of New Sarum, in the county of Wilts," &c., &c., attested by Anthony Thacher as curate.

"Peter Thacher died Feb. 11, 1640." His burial is thus recorded under the date of Feb 19th:

"Burials—Mr. Peter Thacher, Rector, ibm."

His remains were deposited under an altar tomb on the north side of the church yard. It is apparently the most ancient to be found there, and bears this inscription in the first compartment on the south side.

"Here lyeth the bodye of Mr. Peter Thacher, who was a laborious minister of the Gospel of Jesus Christ in ye Parish of St. Edmund for ye space of XIX yeares He departed this lyfe the Lord's Day at three of the clock ye XI of Feb 1640. Let no man move his bones."

He was probably the last of his family buried here, as no inscription appears in the other compartments.

Very respectfully yours,

H. HATCHER.

The same authority speaks of his wife Anne. Their children were as follows:

3 Thomas, born May 1, 1620; died October 15, 1678.

5 Martha, born November —. 1623.* [?]

7 Elizabeth, born January —, 1625.

9 John, born January —, 1627.

11 Samuel, born ———— 1638.

13 Barnabas, born August —, 1640.

We find no records of any of these coming to this country, except *Thomas*, the oldest.

First Generation.† 1-3 THOMAS THACHER, son of the *Rev. Peter*, was born in England, May 1, 1620. In his early minority he appeared to have imbibed true puritan principles. Having received a grammar school education at home, his father intended that his education should have been completed at the university, either of Cambridge or Oxford: but, disgusted with

* It seems to have been the custom of those times to baptize children in infancy, and these dates we have taken from the records of baptism, presuming they were only a week or two old at that time.
† For convenience, and to avoid the confusion consequent upon the use of the same surname in different branches of the family, we have adopted the plan of numbering each member, giving to Peter and his descendants the odd numbers, and to Anthony and his descendants the even numbers. Where two numbers appear before a name the first indicates his or her father.

the prevailing ecclesiastical tyranny to which he must have been subjected, he was induced to decline the proposals of his father, preferring to cross the Atlantic, that he might enjoy liberty of conscience in the wilds of New England. To this determination his parents readily consented, as they themselves intended to have followed him; but this was prevented by the death of his mother. At the age of fifteen years, this enterprising young puritan embarked in a company with his uncle, *Anthony Thacher*, and arrived in New England June 4, 1635. Shortly after their arrival they had occasion to pass from Ipswich to Marblehead. Anthony, with his wife and family embarked on board a bark belonging to Mr. Allerton, of Plymouth; they were overtaken by a tremendous tempest in the night, and shipwrecked on an island in Salem harbor, and twenty-one out of twenty-three persons were drowned, August 14, 1635, Mr. Thacher and his wife being the only persons saved. *Thomas Thacher* "had such a strong and sad impression upon his mind," says Dr. Cotton Mather (Magnalia), "about the issue of the voyage, that he, with another, would needs go by the land, and so escaped perishing with some of his pious and precious friends by sea."* Being thus providentially preserved, young Thacher became an inmate in the family of the Rev. C. Chauncey, who was afterwards president of Harvard College. Under the tuition of that eminent scholar he received his education, and was prepared for the duties of the ministry. He was not long an idle candidate. Such was his pious deportment, and so manifest his qualifications for a Gospel teacher, that he was soon invited to become the pastor of the church at Weymouth, where he was ordained January 2, 1645. In his ministerial labors he was most faithful and affectionate; among his excellencies was a peculiar spirit of prayer, and he was remarkable for the copious, fluent and fervent manner of performing that sacred exercise. Having acquired a knowledge of

---

* This journey was a very hazardous one, it being through an unsettled wilderness, and full of Indians.

medicine, Mr. Thacher united the practice of that profession
with his ecclesiastical vocation, in which he was greatly useful.
He married Eliza, the youngest daughter of the Rev. Ralph
Partridge, the first minister of Duxbury, who, among other
pious ministers was, to use his own expression, "hunted like a
patridge on the mountain," and driven from his native soil to
seek an asylum in this land of religious freedom. She died
June 2, 1664.

His children by his first wife were* [17] Thomas, born ———,
[19] Ralph or Rodolphus, [21] Peter, [23] Patience, [25] Eliza. Patience
married William Kemp of Duxbury, Eliza married Nathaniel
Davenport, the brave captain killed in the great Naragansett
battle, December 19, 1675. For a second husband she married
Samuel Davis, in 1677.

Mr. Thacher married for a second wife Margaret Sheaffe, a
lady belonging in Boston, and became an inhabitant of that
town, where he acquired eminence in the medical profession.
He was conspicuous as a learned divine; and when the third or
old South church was founded, in Boston, he was chosen their
first pastor, and installed February 16, 1670, and continued in
that station till his death, October 15, 1678. Having visited a
patient in a fever, he was himself seized with the disease, which
terminated his existence at the age of fifty-eight years. President Stiles speaks of Mr. Thacher as the best Arabic scholar
known in the country, and states that he composed and published a Hebrew Lexicon. According to Dr. Cotton Mather, he
was a great logician, and well versed in mechanics, both in
theory and practice, and could make all kinds of clockwork to
admiration. In 1677 he published a work entitled a "Brief
Guide in the Small Pox and Measles," which was the first medical work published in America. Mather says he was a most
incomparable scribe; he not only wrote all sorts of hands in the
copy book then extant, with a singular exactness and acuteness,

---

* Savage's Gen. Dic.

but there are yet extant monuments of *Syriac* and other oriental characters of his writing, which are hardly to be imitated. The following elegy by an Indian youth, a student at Harvard College, we find in Mather's Mag. vol. III. p. 152.

AN ELEGY

On the Death of that truly Reverend Man,

THOMAS THACHER,

Who Departed this Life for His Heavenly Home,

October 15, 1678.

I sing of one, though tears bedew the page,
Mourned by the present, as the former age,
Mourned as was Memnon, by Achilles slain,
When o'er his corse, his mother knelt in vain.
Mind, voice, and strength have lost their wonted fire,
As if the muse would weep, but not inspire.
Thacher, 'tis virtue that thy name endears,
Virtue, that climbs beyond the starry spheres.
To men of station, and of low degree,
Thy faith shines forth like beacons o'er the sea.
Though dead, thou livest! victory crowns thy brow,
The grace that saved thee, glorifies thee now ;
Thy cross of suffering thou shalt bear no more,
Temptations, perils, sorrows, all are o'er.
Death, the destroyer, dies—the last of foes—
And life renewed, to life immortal grows.
When the last trumpet, fearfully and loud,
Peals like the thunder through the parted cloud,
And the great Judge of all shall spread his throne,
Thou shalt sit with him as a chosen son;
Then through the skies seek realms of endless day,
To which thy Savior hath prepared the way—
Then 'mid delights for human thought too sweet,
Thy rest is pure—thy pleasure infinite.

Eleazer, an Indian Senior Sophister.

Though the earth contains his dust, his name is yet immortal,
It shall light the future ages, as o'er the past it beamed ;
While his soul, set free from prison, seeks the ever open portal,
Where the shining ones are waiting to welcome the redeemed.

Eleazer.

Second Generation. **3-17** THOMAS, oldest son of *Rev. Thomas* and Eliza P. Thacher, married Mary Savage, daughter of Thos. Savage, and settled in Boston, where he became a successful merchant. He died April 2, 1686, and his widow died July 22, 1730, leaving all her property to her son Peter, who was minister at Weymouth. Their children were:

27 Eliza, born December 26, 1671.
29 Thomas, born September 25, 1673.
31 John, born January 22, 1675.
23 Peter, born 1677.
35 Mary, born January 28, 1680.

3-19 RALPH, or RODOLPHUS, second son of *Rev. Thomas.* married January 1, 1670, Ruth, daughter of George Partridge, of Duxbury, where he lived several years. He was constable, 1678, and clerk of the town several years from 1685, but his benevolence carried him to Chilmark, Martha's Vineyard, where he settled in the ministry and preached many years. "In June, 1711, he gave to his son Rodolphus alias Ralph, an estate of sixty acres."* His children were:

37 Thomas, born October 9, 1670.
39 Eliza, born March 1, 1672.
41 Ann,¹ born November 26, 1673.   Died young.
43 Ruth, born November 1, 1675.
45 Rodolphus, born January 9, 1678.
47 Lydia, born January 24, 1680—(married Jonathan Peterson, of Chilmark, and died May 26, 1756.)
49 Mary, born March 8, 1682.
51 Ann,² born March 30, 1684.
53 Peter, born August 17, 1686.
Little is known of his life, but his descendants are numerous.

3-21 PETER, the youngest son of *Rev. Thomas*, was born July 18, 1651, at Salem; graduated at Harvard College 1671; was

* Mather's Magnalia, Vol. 1., page 27.

ordained over the church in Milton, June 1, 1681. He married, November 21, 1677, Theodora Oxenbridge, daughter of Rev. John Oxenbridge; she died November 18, 1697. For a second wife he married Susannah Bailey, widow of Rev. John Bailey; she died September 4, 1724, in her fifty-ninth year. He died December 17, 1727, aged seventy-seven years, having been the honored and beloved pastor of the church at Milton nearly forty-seven years. His children by his first wife were:

[55] Theodora, born ——.

[57] Bathsheba ——.

[59] Oxenbridge, born May 17, 1681; died October 22, 1772.

[61] Eliza, born March 7, 1682; married Rev. Samuel Niles; died February 10, 1715.

[63] Mary, born ——.

[65] Peter, born October 16, 1688; died April 22, 1744.

[67] John,[1] died young.

[69] Thomas, born ——, 1693; died ——, 1721.

[71] John,[2] born ——.

Of [29] Thomas and [31] John, sons of [17] Thomas, merchant, at Boston, we have no record.

[17-38] PETER, youngest son of *Thomas*, of Boston, was born in August, 1677, graduated at Harvard in 1696, married Hannah Curwin, October 14, 1708, ordained as minister at Weymouth November 26, 1707, having, in 1723, received a call to settle as pastor of the New North Church in Boston. About fifty members of that church and congregation were dissatisfied that the invitation should be given to Mr. Thacher, who was then the settled minister of Weymouth, and that he should leave his flock. "They separated from the society and built a new meeting-house, which received the name of Revenge. At the time they met to instal him, the disturbance was so great that the services could not be regularly performed. After a public declaration of the majority of the society in the meeting-house, that they accepted Mr. Thacher, the moderator announced him to be

their minister, and the meeting broke up." He died March 1. 1739, leaving no children.

Third Generation. ⁷⁹⁻³⁷ THOMAS, the oldest son of *Rev. Ralph*, of Martha's Vineyard, was born October 9, 1670; married November 16, 1704, to Mary Deane. Their children were:

⁹³ Rodolphus or Ralph, born August, 1709; died 1728.

⁹⁵ Ruth, born February 18, 1711.

⁹⁷ Partridge, born August, 1714.

⁹⁹ Mary, born April 20, 1717.

¹⁰¹ Annie, born March 29, 1720.

⁷⁹⁻⁴⁵ Of RALPH, or RODOLPHUS, second son of *Rev. Ralph*, we have no further record.

⁷⁹⁻⁵³ PETER, youngest son of *Rev. Ralph*, of Martha's Vineyard, was born August 17, 1686, married in 1713 to Abigail Hibbard, of Windham, Connecticut, then of the age of fifteen, a woman of remarkable beauty, as was her mother, whose maiden name was Abigail Lindon, of Rhode Island, and who was an aunt of Josiah Lindon, Governor of Rhode Island in 1768. They settled in Lebanon, Conn., where he died, February 1766, aged eighty. His wife, Abigail, died there July 9, 1778, aged eighty. They had children, as follows:

¹¹³ Peter, born April 28, 1716; died August 24, 1751, at Providence, R I.

¹¹⁵ John,' born August 9, 1719; died April 3, 1739.

¹¹⁷ Lydia, born December 17, 1720, married John Davidson, of Mansfield, Connecticut; died June 9, 1792.

¹¹⁹ Joseph, born October 11, 1722; died ——, at Lebanon.

¹²¹ Abigail, born June 20, 1725, unmarried. She adopted the orphan children of her brother Rodolphus—Stephen and Mary, upon his decease. Upon the marriage of Stephen, she became an inmate of his family at Kennebunk, Maine, and resided with him till her decease, July 21, 1813, aged ninety years.

[123] Ruth, born May 27, 1727, married —— Goodwin, of Lebanon ; died ——.

[125] Rodolphus,[1] born April 2, 1729; died ——, 1740.

[127] Samuel, born May 1, 1730; died 1812 in New York city.

[129] Josiah, born July 8, 1733; died December 14, 1799.

[131] Jared, born March 5, 1735; died in the "French war," and was interred on an island in the Hudson river near Fort Edward.

[133] Ebenezer, born April 2, 1738; died ——, 1740.

[135] John,[2] born February 22, 1739; died October 7, 1805.

[137] Rodolphus.[2] born March 12, 1742; died August 6, 1788.

Third Generation. [21-59] OXENBRIDGE, the oldest son of *Rev. Peter,* of Milton, was born May 17, 1679, and graduated at Cambridge in 1698. He for many years sustained the office of selectman, in the town of Boston, and representative to the general court, but removed to Milton, his native place, and, for several years was a representative of that town. He devoted some part of his early life to the ministry, and preached the first sermon that was delivered to the settlers of Punkapog, now Stoughton. One of the old settlers of the place, in a kind of rapture, addressed the Rev. Thomas Thacher, of Dedham, upon hearing him preach, "Your grandfather, Oxenbridge, was the first man that brought a Bible among us." He died October 19, 1772, aged ninety-three years. He had a son, [139] *Oxenbridge, Jr.,* born 1720; died July 8, 1765.

[21-65] PETER, Jr., second son of *Rev. Peter,* of Milton, was born in that town October 6, 1688, graduated at Harvard in 1706, ordained at Middleboro' November 2, 1709, married Mary, daughter of Samuel Prince, of Sandwich, and had ten children, among whom were Mary, Oxenbridge, Samuel and [161] Peter, born January 26, 1716; died 1785. He died April 22, 1744, aged fifty-six years, having sustained a ministerial character of great respectability, and received a large number of members into his church during the later years of his ministry.

Of [69] Thomas and [71] John. sons of [21] Peter. of Milton, we have no record.

[53-129] JOSIAH, son of *Peter*, of Lebanon, was born July 8. 1733, married July 13, 1768. to Apphia Mayo. He was a graduate of Princeton College, and settled in the ministry at Gorham, Maine. He subsequently left the ministry, and was a Representative, Senator and Councillor of Massachusetts, and a Judge of the Court of Common Pleas of that State. He died December 14, 1799. His wife died October —, 1807. Their children were as follows:

[201] Peter,[1] born July 13, 1769; died August 8, 1769.

[203] Apphia,[1] born August 19, 1770; died September 3, 1770.

[205] Peter,[2] born August 5, 1771: died January 2, 1772.

[207] Apphia,[2] born March 23, 1773: died January 30, 1782.

[209] Peter,[3] born July 24, 1774; died January —, 1811.

[211] Mary, born May 8, 1776; died June —. 1789.

[213] Faith, born October 30, 1778; died June 23, 1816.

[215] John, born February 18, 1781: died January 3, 1810.

[217] Apphia,[3] born April 7, 1785, married Rev. Reuben Nason, for many years Preceptor of Gorham Academy, and had one child who died unmarried. She died August 12. 1808.

[219] Josiah, born January 21, 1789; died August 23, 1807.

[53-135] JOHN, son of *Peter*, was born February 22, 1739. married Abigail Swift, of Lebanon, Connecticut. At the age of forty-eight he removed to Lempster, New Hampshire, and died there October 7, 1805. Their children were:

[221] Jared, [223] Peter, [225] James, [227] John, [229] Lydia, [231] Abigail, [233] Paulina, [235] Nancy. All of them, except Peter, it is believed, removed to the State of New York, and all, it is said, lived in Ontario county, except James, who settled in Chatauqua county. The most of them lived in Hopewell. formerly Easton.

[223] Peter settled in Hartford, Connecticut, and is deceased. He was the father of the distinguished Prof. Thomas Anthony

Thacher, of Yale College, and of Rev. George Thacher, President of Iowa University; also of Sheldon P. Thacher, Esq., of Hartford, and other sons and daughters.

33-137 RODOLPHUS, youngest son of *Peter*, was born March 12. 1742, at Lebanon, Connecticut, married Mary Cone, and lived and died at Lebanon August 6, 1788, aged forty-six. His wife died October 24, 1775, aged thirty-three. He never again married. They had two children.

237 Stephen, born January 9, 1774; died February 19, 1859.

239 Mary, born ——, 1776; died at Lebanon May 23, 1794.

Fourth Generation. 39-139 OXENBRIDGE, Jr., son of *Rev. Oxenbridge*, was born in Milton in 1720, and graduated at Cambridge College in 1738; died July 8, 1765, aged forty-five years, and was, at the time of his death, one of the four representatives in the general court for the town of Boston. This gentleman died in the midst of his merited reputation and usefulness, being a lawyer of great eminence, and a learned and able writer. He was distinguished for his patriotic spirit and amiable moral character, which are still remembered. Governor Hutchinson, in his History of Massachusetts, speaks of him as an active and influential opposer of the measures of Parliament, about the period of the stamp act. His name has frequently been mentioned in terms of high esteem, as a compeer with Adams, Quincy and Otis. He published two pamphlets; one in 1760, on the *Gold Coin;* another in 1764. " *The Sentiments of a British American, occasioned by an act to lay certain duties on the British Colonies and Plantations.*"

He had four children, as follows :

275 Peter, born March 21, 1752; died December 16, 1802.

277 Thomas, born 1756; died 1812.

279 Nathaniel.

281 Bathsheba, married December 25, 1769, to Jeremiah Dummer, of Boston, and had seven children, one of whom, Jeremiah, Jr., was a teacher to Lord Byron for a time.

[65-149] PETER, son of *Rev. Peter*, of Middleboro', was born January 25, 1716, graduated at Harvard University in 1737, ordained at Attleboro' November 30, 1748. He was the first minister who preached in the east or second parish in that town, and he preached there about five years previous to his being ordained. He was one of ten children, and the oldest of seven sons. According to family tradition, he was the fourteenth oldest son in succession, employed in the work of the gospel ministry, a remarkable circumstance. Mr. Thacher was a man of great simplicity and plainness of manners, a worthy and useful minister, and his memory is justly revered. "A small volume of his sermons was published some time after his death, but, although the sentiment may be preserved, an unjustifiable liberty was taken with his language. However plain may be the style of a man, no material posthumous alteration ought to take place in preparing his works for the public. Every one appears most natural in his own garb. The only publication extant, so far as the author of this work* knows, which exhibits a fair specimen of Mr. Thacher's common, plain and impressive manner of sermonizing, is the discourse occasioned by the death of his much esteemed friend, the Rev. Habijah Weld, of Attleboro'." Mr. Thacher continued to be highly useful in the ministry, contributing greatly to the welfare and prosperity of his people, till, being seized with a palsy, which rendered him unable to perform the duties of his office, he was dismissed by a vote of the parish. He died September 13, 1785, in the seventieth year of his age, and forty-third of his ministry.

He was married in 1749 to Bethia, daughter of Deacon Obadiah Carpenter, of Attleboro'. They had seven sons and three daughters, among whom were:

[283] Obadiah, [285] Peter, and [287] Nancy, who married John Tyler, whose grandson, William S. Tyler, is now Professor at Amherst College, Massachusetts.

---

* Alden's Col. Epitaphs.

Fifth Generation. ¹⁴⁹⁻²⁸⁵ *Deacon* PETER, son of *Rev. Peter*, of Attleboro', married Nanne Tyler, and had a son Peter, also a deacon, who has sons, Peter *Thatcher*, of Cleveland, and William T. Thacher, of Boston.

¹³⁷⁻²³⁷ *Hon.* STEPHEN, only son of *Rodolphus*, graduated at Yale College in 1795, being a class-mate of his life-long friend, President Day. He was educated for the ministry, but relinquished it on account of feeble health. He settled at Kennebunk, Maine, in 1803, where he was engaged in trade for some years. He was an ardent supporter of Mr. Jefferson, and took a very active and influential part in the political controversies of the day. July 4, 1803, he delivered an oration which was published, and which Mr. Jefferson, in an autograph letter to the author, now in the possession of the Maine Historical Society, highly complimented. In 1807 Governor Sullivan appointed him Judge of Probate for the county of York, which office he filled with great acceptance until his resignation in 1818, to enter upon the duties of the Collectorship of Passamaquody, to which he was appointed by President Monroe. In 1810, he was appointed Postmaster of Kennebunk, and was continued in that office as long as he resided there. In 1818, he removed to Lubec, Maine, and assumed the duties of the collectorship, which he retained to the end of his third term, in 1830. He removed to Rockland, Maine, in 1856, where several of his sons then resided, and there died, February 19, 1859, aged eighty-five.

September 4, 1804, he was married to Harriet Preble, of York, Maine, a sister of Hon. William P. Preble, a Judge of the Supreme Court of Maine, and Ambassador of the United States to the King of the Netherlands. She was a lady of distinguished excellence. She died at Lubec, December 25, 1849, aet. sixty-five. Their children were as follows:

²⁵³ George Washington, born August 31, 1805; never married; resided many years in New York City; died at Rockland, Maine, November 20, 1864.

[255] Peter, born October 14. 1810: married Margaret Louisa Potter. of Portland, April 26. 1841. They have children. five daughters, four sons.

[257] Mary. born May 10, 1812: married October 18. 1837, William B. Smith, of Machias, Maine: died May 19. 1838.

[259] Emily Bliss, born June 5, 1814: married Edmund A. Souder, of Philadelphia, July 28, 1834. They have children, four daughters, three sons.

[261] Joseph Storer, born August 31, 1816: died October 24, 1818.

[263] Ralph Partridge Preble, born September 6. 1818: died September 13, 1825.

[265] Harriet Preble, born October 19, 1820; married May 11, 1846, to Edward Mellus, of Salem; died December 25, 1855. Her husband died at Fouchou, China, August 11, 1856.

[267] Priscilla Josephine, born August 31. 1823: died August 25, 1844.

[269] Joseph Anderson, born April 25, 1825: married at Zembrota, Minnesota, August 28, 1859, to Nancy A. Wilder, of that place: children, six.

[271] Ralph Partridge Emilius, born September 7, 1826; graduate of Yale College.

[273] Abigail Lindon, born March 4, 1830.

[139_275] PETER, D. D., the eldest son of *Oxenbridge, Jr.*, was born March 21, 1752, at Milton, his parents having retired there, on account of the small pox being in Boston. His father died when he was thirteen years old. His juvenile years afforded the highest promise of eminence as a divine, manifesting in his deportment an uncommon share of gravity, and a preference for books of piety, and the conversation of religious persons, to childish amusements. He was admitted a student of Harvard College when a youth, and received his college honors in the year 1769, at the early age of seventeen years and four months. He soon acquired extraordinary qualifications for the duties of the ministry, and no sooner commenced preaching than he was desired to supply the pulpit in Malden, and on September 19, 1710, was ordained pastor over the church in that place. He was distinguished for his oratorical powers and ardor in the pulpit; his voice was peculiarly melodious, and in his public devotions his fluency and fervor were so impressive, that he seldom failed to produce general admiration and applause. He was not less remarkable for his colloquial powers, which were admirably adapted to disseminate pleasure and instruction. In early life Dr. Thacher was in principle a rigid Calvinist, and the celebrated Whitfield embraced him as a well qualified advocate for the cause of Orthodoxy; but he gradually abated his rigid tenets, and, in riper years, became catholic and charitable towards other denominations of Christians; and such was his liberality, such his kind and gentlemanly deportment, that all classes of Christians enjoyed satisfaction and pleasure in holding intercourse with him. Bigotry and excessive zeal met his unequivocal disapprobation. On the commencement of the controversy between the American colonies and our English ancestry, Dr. Thacher was found among the first of those divines who with zeal espoused the noble cause of freedom. Not satisfied with his exemplary efforts in the line of his profession, public addresses, and influential conversation, he actually joined a military corps, and shouldered his musket for the combat; but he was not permitted to depart from home, where his services were indispensable. On the 5th of March, 1770, by the request of the people of Boston, he pronounced, at Watertown, the oration against "*Standing Armies*," which had been annually delivered, in the Old South Church, in commemoration of the Boston massacre. Here his superior talents and brilliant intellectual energies were conspicuous, as on all public occasions allotted to him in his sphere of useful labors.

When, in the year 1780, a convention assembled to form a constitution for our commonwealth, Dr. Thacher was chosen a member of that honorable body for the town of Malden, and few were more active or more influential. He was afterwards warmly attached to, and a strenuous supporter of, the constitution, and was also among the warmest admirers of the Constitution of the United States.

In 1785, Dr. Thacher became the pastor of the Brattle Street church in Boston, where he was installed January 12. The officiating ministers were, the Rev. David Osgood, of Medford, who preached the sermon, Dr. Lathrop, who gave the charge, and Dr. Clark the right hand of fellowship. In this enlarged sphere of ecclesiastical functions, he acquired much honor and celebrity. The University of Edinburgh honored him with the degree of Doctor of Divinity, and several divines, to whom his character was known, in Europe, manifested their respect for him, by appointing him a member of the Society for Propagating the Gospel among the Indians in North America. He was an active member of this Board, and also with the society connected with it, and was for several years their secretary. He was one of the earliest members of the Historical Society, and one of its Committee for Publications. He was also elected a member of the American Academy of Arts and Sciences, and of almost all the literary and charitable institutions existing in New England; in which his industry and influence were conspicuous and impressive. He was uncommonly well versed in the history of his own and foreign countries, both civil and ecclesiastical, and possessed a large share of puritanical zeal, ever opposed to *prelatic power*, and an ardent advocate for the support of good New England principles. He was a man of singular integrity, urbane and courteous in manners, facetious in conversation, and fond of anecdote. As a friend he was affectionate, kind, and benevolent.

In the year 1802, Dr. Thacher finding his health on the decline, and a pulmonary complaint becoming alarming, was, by advice of physicians induced to repair to the State of Georgia, with the hope of deriving benefit from a milder climate. His people, anxious to contribute all in their power to his relief, cheerfully defrayed the expense of the voyage; but such was the rapid progress of his disease, that he died in the city of Savannah on the 10th of December, about six weeks after leaving Boston. Whether abroad among strangers, or at home surrounded by familiar friends, Dr. Thacher constantly received marks of respect and sympathy, and the most cordial affection in life and in death ; and his character has been eulogized both in prose and verse.

"The father and grandfather of Dr. Thacher had been preachers of the gospel before they entered other professions. An old lady of Milton recollected hearing sermons from Thachers of five generations in direct succession. Mr. Thacher, of Milton, his son and grandson, Oxenbridge ; the late Dr. Thacher and his son, the minister of Lynn ; besides collateral branches of the family." It may be added that there has never been a time since the first Thomas and Antony, without ministers bearing the name of Thacher in New England.

Dr. Thacher married Mrs. Elizabeth Poole, October 8, 1770, by whom he had ten children, as follows :

351 Thomas C., born October 11, 1771; died September 24, 1849.

353 Peter,[1] born December 1, 1772 ; died September 6, 1775.

355 Sarah, born ——, 1774 ; died young.

357 Joseph Warren, born July 4, 1775; died March 19, 1809.

359 Peter O., born December 22, 1776; died February 22, 1843.

361 Charles,[1] born September 12, 1779; died November 13, 1779.

363 Sarah,[2] born October 5, 1781 ; died January 13, 1802.

365 Mary Harvey, born March 27, 1783 ; died June 24, 1849.

367 Samuel Cooper, born December 14, 1785 ; died January 2, 1818.

369 Charles,[2] born June 15, 1787 ; died May 18, 1823.

139-277 THOMAS, second son of *Oxenbridge, Jr.*, and brother of *Peter, D. D.*, was born in 1756, graduated at Harvard in 1775, and was ordained pastor of the second church at Dedham. He was a man of sound understanding, respectable in his profession, liberal in his views, and in good fellowship with his Christian brethren. He was not polished in his manners, nor did he possess partiality enough for the other sex to enter into the connubial state. He spent his life with his people, and died, lamented, October 18, 1812, aged fifty-six.

[130-279] NATHANIEL, youngest son of *Oxenbridge, Jr.*, was a subaltern officer in the American army. He also died a bachelor.

Sixth Generation. [273-351] THOMAS CUSHING, oldest son of *Peter, D. D.*, was born at Malden, October 11, 1771, graduated at Harvard in 1790, was ordained as minister of the first parish in Lynn, August 13, 1794, in which capacity he served with great acceptance until 1813, when he removed to Cambridge, Massachusetts, where he died September 24, 1849. He married Elizabeth Blaney, who survived him, living until September, 1858, when she died at South Reading, aged eighty-eight. Their children were:

[371] Charles Oxenbridge, born ——, died unmarried, aged 32.

[373] Peter Oxenbridge, born ——, died ——, aged 7.

[375] Hannah B——, born ——, married Reuben P. Washburne, of Leicester, and had five children, among whom were Peter T. Washburne. lately Governor of Vermont, and John S. Washburne, a lawyer in New York city.

[377] Mary, married Edward G. Stevens, of Boston.

[379] Eliza, married same one after the death of her sister.

[275-353] PETER OXENBRIDGE, son of *Peter, D. D.*, was born at Malden, December 22, 1776, graduated at Harvard 1796, was appointed Judge of the Municipal Court in Boston in 1823, in which office he served for twenty years, much respected for his integrity and humanity. He died at Cambridge, September 24, 1849. He married Miss Parkman (sister of Dr. Parkman, of Boston), and had children, among whom were:

[401] Joseph S. Buckminster, of Natchez, Mississippi.

[403] George McDonough (late Danish Consul in Boston), born 1809; died June 2, 1858.

SAMUEL COOPER, son of *Peter*, D. D., was born December 14, 1785. From early life he exhibited those qualities of mind which are so very desirable in a teacher of religion, and in riper years he determined to enter a profession which his father before him had followed and adorned. He was admitted a student at the University in Cambridge, in the year 1800, and graduated with its highest honors in 1804. He immediately commenced his theological studies in Boston, and enjoyed the valuable privilege of having them directed by the Rev. Dr. Channing. In the year 1806 he accompanied his friend, the Rev. Mr. Buckminster, on a voyage to Europe. Soon after his return he accepted the office of Librarian of Harvard College, and entered on its duties in 1808. On the third of November, 1810, the Rev. J. T. Kirkland was inducted President of Harvard University, and on this occasion Mr. Thacher was appointed to deliver a congratulatory address in Latin. Many then present remarked the graceful appearance of the orator, and his address received praises from all lips, for the propriety of its sentiments and the elegance of its Latinity.

But the time approached when he was to leave his employment at Cambridge for a sphere of higher and more arduous duties. He received a call from the society of the New South Church, in Boston, of which President Kirkland had been the minister, and was ordained May 15. He now lived only for his people, and directed all his exertions for the promotion of their good. But soon a melancholy cloud rose up, and threw its shade over the morning prospect of his usefulness. He was not gifted with a constitution sufficiently vigorous to support him for any length of time, under the manifold labors of his profession, and in the spring of the year after his settlement, he found it necessary to take a journey for the benefit of his declining health. A free use of the waters of Saratoga Springs, was so beneficial to him, that, after remaining there some days, he set out on his return to Boston, with renewed strength and hopes. But on arriving at Worcester, he was attacked with raising blood from the lungs, which immediately reduced him to a state of extreme debility. He gradually recovered, so far as to believe himself able to recommence his ministerial duties. In the autumn of 1815 he was severely attacked by a return of hemorrhage from the lungs, and in the spring it was determined by his physicians that he should take a voyage to Europe. In August Mr. Thacher once more bade farewell to his home, not as before, for the purpose of watching over the health of a friend, but with the hope of recovering his own. On his arrival in London, he consulted Dr. Baillie, physician to the king, and Dr. Wells. The place selected for his winter's residence was not such an one as his inclination would have chosen; for though it bore the name of Promise, it was far removed, not only from his friends, but from the civilized portions of the world. "I am on the point of embarking," he writes, "for the Cape of Good Hope. I am led to this measure by finding the opinions of the most eminent physicians here coincide with that of Dr. Jackson and my other medical friends at home. Of course it would have been more pleasing to me to have been recommended to some spot less distant from you all. But I came abroad, not from pleasure or curiosity, but in order, by God's blessing, to regain the ability of being useful, I am bound to take that course which shall seem to lead most directly to this object."

He arrived at the Cape January 1st, 1817, where he remained, though without deriving much benefit from the climate, till the 5th of April. A boisterous voyage proved highly injurious to his health, and, on his arrival in London, the physicians were of opinion that he ought not to return home. He gave up his own wishes to what appeared his duty, and dooming himself to a longer absence from his country and friends, sought out once more a retreat for the winter. He went to Paris in August, and, after a residence of a few weeks, proceeded to Moulins, on account of its great reputation for the mildness of its climate. His health declined from the time of his arrival in

France; and though he himself had constant hopes of his recovery, and return to America, the friends who had opportunities of seeing him, perceived that, in all probability, the time of his final rest was at hand. He died at Moulins January 1st, 1818.

"Mr. Thacher's piety was indeed the most perfect feature of his character. It appeared to control and guide his principles, his actions, his conversation and his manners. It seemed to take the place of judgment and will, to rule in his mind as it did in his heart. In short it would be impossible to give an idea of his character, without taking into view this ruling principle; for he was one whose submission to the will of God, sense of dependence on him, and trust in the promises of the Gospel, were so constant and ardent, that they gave a peculiar holiness, purity and sweetness to all that he said and did."

The following extract from a sketch of his character, by the Rev. Dr. Channing, will further exhibit the nature of Mr. Thacher's piety:

"It was warm but not heated; earnest, but tranquil; a habit not an impulse; the air which he breathed, not a tempestuous wind, giving occasional violence to his motions. A constant dew seemed to distil on him from heaven, giving freshness to his devout sensibilities; but it was a gentle influence, seen not in its falling but in its fruits. His piety appeared chiefly in gratitude and submission, sentiments peculiarly suited to such a mind as his. He felt strongly that God had crowned his life with peculiar goodness; and yet, when his blessings were withdrawn his acquiescence was as deep and sincere as his thankfulness. His devotional exercises in public, were particularly striking. He came to the mercy-seat as one who was not a stranger there. He seemed to inherit from his venerable father the gift of prayer. His acts of adoration discovered a mind penetrated by the majesty of God; but his sublime conceptions of these attributes were always tempered and softened by a sense of the divine benignity. The *paternal character* of God was not only his belief, but had become a part of his mind. He never forgot that he worshipped the *father:* his firm conviction of the strict and proper unity of the divine nature, taught him to unite and concentrate, in his conception of the Father, all that is lovely and attractive, as well as all that is solemn and venerable; and the general effect of his prayers was to diffuse a devout calmness, a filial confidence over the minds of his pious hearers.

"His deportment in private and social life was remarkably gentle and engaging, and, at the same time, dignified. They who were led by his mildness and affability to think that he might be too nearly or familiarly approached, were sure to be deceived. There was a line drawn about him, unseen, but not to be passed over, which repelled rudeness or levity. He won, without effort, the affection of friendship, and made himself the object of respectful attachment, both at home and abroad. His temper was calm and even, for his heart was the dwelling of piety and peace. His ashes repose in a foreign land. His friends are deprived of the melancholy gratification of paying their frequent visits to his tomb. The peasant of France passes carelessly by it, and knows not how cherished and excellent was he, whose remains it covers. The weeds may grow round it, and the long grass may wave over it, for there is none to pluck them away. But his memory is sacredly kept in many a heart, and there stands a monument to his name more lasting than marble, in the good which he effected while living, and in the example which he has left behind him "

The foregoing is an abstract of an interesting memoir prefixed to a volume of Mr. Thacher's sermons.

²⁷⁵⁻²⁶⁵ CHARLES, youngest son of *Peter, D. D.*, born at Malden June 15, 1787, was an honorable and successful merchant at Boston, and died, greatly lamented, May 18, 1832, of pulmonary consumption. He had a son, Charles, died unmarried a few years since.

We have no further *definite* records of this branch of the family, though the latter generations are very numerous.

———— •• ————

SECOND BRANCH.

First Generation. ² ANTONY* THACHER, a brother of *Rev. Peter Thacher*, came from Salisbury, England. The name of the father of Antony and Peter is not known, nor is the place of their birth, but it is supposed to have been Somersetshire. Besides these two brothers, there were Clement, William, Thomas, John, Anne (who married Christopher Batt), and Dorothy, who

* Mr. Thacher spelled his given name *Antony*, as appears from papers containing his signature, eight of which, to our knowledge, are preserved. We, therefore, in speaking of him, spell it as he did, for he, being an educated man, it is to be supposed knew best how to spell his own name.

married Richard Sears, and was in this country in 1682, settling at Sesuet (now East Dennis), Massachusetts, and from whom have descended a numerous family. In the will of his brother Thomas, which is dated January 8, 1610, he is spoken of as being in *the separation*, and residing in Holland. To have taken such a decided stand in religion as is indicated in the will, he must have been at least sixteen, so there is no doubt that he was born previous to 1595. He served occasionally (from 1631 to 1634), as curate for his brother, who was rector of St. Edmunds in Salisbury. He embarked for America on the 6th of April, 1635, at Southampton, in the "James," of London, and arrived at Ipswich June 4. In the ship's clearance he is called a "*Tayler*," probably for deception. Besides his own family, he was probably accompanied by his cousin, Rev. Joseph Avery, with his wife and six children, and his nephew, Thomas Thacher, and a servant, Peter Higden; but of all these, only the names of Antony and Higden appear on the list of passengers.

After remaining a short time at Ipswich, his cousin Avery received an invitation to preach at Marblehead, and they, with their respective families (except his nephew Thomas, then fifteen years old, who preferred land travel), embarked for that place August 11, 1635, and were wrecked off Cape Ann, and all but Antony and his wife were drowned. A full account of this shipwreck is given in the following letter from Antony to his brother Peter, written a few days after the occurrence.

"I must turn my drowned pen and shaking hand to indite the story of such sad news as never before this happened in *New England*. There was a league of perpetual friendship between my cousin Avery and myself, never to forsake each other to the death, but to be partakers of each other's misery or welfare, as also of habitation in the same place. Now upon our arrival at New England, there was an offer made unto us My cousin Avery was invited to *Marblehead* to be their pastor in due time; there being no church planted there as yet, but a town appointed to set up the trade of fishing. Because many there (the most being fishermen) were something loose and remiss in their behavior, my cousin Avery was unwilling to go thither, and so refusing, we went to *Newbury*, intending there to sit down. But being solicited so often, both by the men of the place and by the magistrates, and by Mr. Cotton, and most of the ministers, who alleged what a benefit we might be to the people there, and also to the country and commonwealth, at length we embraced it, and thither consented to go They of *Marblehead* forthwith sent a pinnace for us and our goods. We embarked at *Ipswich*, August 11, 1635, with our families and substance, bound for *Marblehead*, we being in all twenty-three souls, viz.: eleven in my cousin's family, seven in mine, and one Mr. William Elliot sometime of *New Sarum*, and four mariners. The next morning, having commended ourselves to God with cheerful hearts, we hoisted sail; but the Lord suddenly turned our cheerfulness into mourning and lamentations, for, on the fourteenth of August, 1635, about ten at night, having a fresh gale of wind, our sails being old and done, were split, the mariners, because that it was night, would not put to her new sails, but resolved to cast anchor till the morning. But before daylight it pleased the Lord to send so mighty a storm as the like was never known in *New England* since the English came, nor in the memory of any of the Indians. It was so furious that our anchor came home, whereupon the mariners let out more cable, which slipped away. Then our sailors knew not what to do; but we were driven before the wind and waves. My cousin and I perceived our danger, and solemnly recommended ourselves to God, the Lord both of earth and seas, expecting with every wave to be swallowed up and drenched in the deep; and as my cousin, his wife, and my tender babes sat comforting and cheering one the other in the Lord against ghastly death, which every moment stared us in the face, and sat triumphing upon each one's forehead, we were, by the violence of the waves and the fury of the winds (by the Lord's permission), lifted up upon a rock, between two high rocks, yet all was one rock, but it raged with the stroke which came into the pinnace, so as we were presently up to our middles in water as we sat. The waves came furiously and violently over us and against us, but by reason of the rocks' position could not lift us off, but beat her all to pieces.

"Now look with me on our distress and consider of my misery, who beheld the ship broken and the water in her, and violently overwhelming us; my goods and provisions swimming in the seas, my friends almost drowned, and mine own poor children so untimely (if I may so term it without offence), before mine eyes, drowned and ready to be swallowed up and dashed to pieces against the rocks by the merciless waves, and myself ready to accompany them. But I must go on to an end of this woeful relation. In the same room whereat he sat, the master of the pinnace not knowing what to do, our foremast was cut down, our mainmast broken in three pieces, the fore part of the pinnace beat away, our goods swimming about the seas, my children bewailing me as not pitying themselves and myself bemoaning them, poor souls, whom I had occasioned to such an end in their tender years, when as they could scarce be sensible of death. And so likewise my cousin, his wife and his children, and both of us bewailing each other, in our Lord and only Saviour, Jesus Christ, in whom only we had comfort and cheerfulness insomuch that from the greatest to the least of us, there was not one screech or outcry made, but all as silent sheep, were contentedly resolved to die together lovingly, as since our acquaintance we had lived together friendly. Now as I was sitting in the cabin room door, with my body in the room, when lo, one of the sailors by a wave, being washed out of the pinnace, was gotten in again, and coming into the cabin room over my back, cried out, 'We are all cast away, the Lord have mercy upon us. I have been washed overboard into the sea and gotten in again.' His speech made me look forth and looking towards the sea, and seeing how we were, I turned myself to my cousin and the rest, and spake these words—'Oh, cousin, it hath pleased God to cast us here between two rocks, the shore not far off from us, for I saw the tops of trees when I looked forth ' Whereupon the master of the pinnace, looking up to the scuttle-hole of the quarter deck, went out at it, but I never saw him afterward. Then he that had been in the sea went out again by me and leaped overboard towards the rocks, whom afterwards also I could not see. Now none were left in the barque that I knew or saw, but my cousin, his wife and children, myself and mine and his maid servant. But my cousin thought I would have fled from him, and said unto me, 'Oh, cousin, leave me not, let us die together,' and reached forth his hand unto me. Then I, letting go my son Peter's hand, took him by the hand and said : ' Cousin, I purpose it not; whither shall I go? I am willing and ready here to die with you and my poor children. God be merciful to us and receive us to himself,' adding these words, ' the Lord is able and willing to help and deliver us ' He replied, saying, ' True, cousin, but what His pleasure is, we know not ; I fear we have been too unthankful for former deliverances, but he hath promised to deliver us from sin and condemnation, and bring us safe to heaven, through the all-sufficient satisfaction of Jesus Christ ; this therefore we may challenge of him.' To which I, replying, said ' that is all the deliverance I now desire and expect,' which words I no sooner said, but by a mighty wave I was with a piece of the barque, washed out upon part of the rock where the wave left me, almost drowned ; but recovering my feet, I saw above me on the rock, my daughter Mary, to whom I had no sooner gotten, but my cousin Avery and his eldest son came to us, being all four of us washed out by one and the same wave. We went all to a small hole on the top of the rock, whence we called to those in the pinnace to come unto us, supposing we had been in more safety then than they were in. My wife seeing us there crept up into the scuttle of the quarter deck to come unto us ; but presently came another wave, and dashing the pinnace all to pieces, carried my wife away in the scuttle as she was, with the greater part of the quarter-deck unto the shore, where she was cast safely but her legs was something bruised, and much timber of the vessel being there also cast, she was sometime before she could get away, being washed by the waves. All the rest that were in the barque were drowned in the merciless seas. We four by that wave were clean swept away from off the rock also, into the sea, the Lord in one instant of time disposing of fifteen souls of us according to his good pleasure and will. His pleasure and wonderful great mercy to me was thus : Standing on the rock as before you heard, with my eldest daughter, my cousin and his eldest son, looking upon and talking to them in the barque, whenas we were by that merciless wave washed off the rock, as before you heard, God in his mercy caused me to fall by the stroke of the wave, flat on my face, for my face was towards the sea, insomuch that I was sliding off the rock into the sea, the Lord directed my toes into a joint of the rock's sides, as also the tops of some of my fingers, with my right hand, by means whereof, the wave leaving me I remained so, having in the rock only my head above the water, when on the left hand I espied a board or plank of the pinnace. And as I was reaching out my left hand to lay hold on it, by another coming over the top of the rock. I was washed away from the rock, and by the violence of the waves was driven hither and thither in the seas a great while, and had many dashes against the rocks. At length, past hopes of life, and wearied in body and in spirit, I even gave over to nature, and being ready to receive in the waters of death, I lifted up both my heart and hand to the God of heaven (for note), I had my senses remaining perfect with me all the time that I was under and in the water, who at that instant lifted my head above the top of the water that so I might breathe without any hindrance by the waters. I stood bolt upright as if I had stood upon my feet, but I felt no bottom, nor had any footing for to stand upon, but the waters. While I was thus above the water, I saw by me a piece of the mast, as I suppose, about three feet long, which I labored to catch into my arms. But suddenly I was overwhelmed with water and driven to and fro again, and at last I felt the ground with my right foot, when immediately, whilst I was thus groveling on my face, I presently, recovering my feet was in the water up to my breast, and through God's great mercy, had my face unto the shore, and not to the sea. I made haste to get out but was thrown down on my hands with the waves, and so with safety crept to the dry shore, where, blessing God, I turned about to look for my children and friends, but saw neither nor any part of the pinnace where I left them as I supposed. But I saw my wife about a butt length from me getting herself forth from amongst the timber of the broken barque. But before I could get to her she was gotten to the shore. I was in the water after I was washed from the rock before I came to the shore, a quarter of an hour at least. When we were come each to the other we went and sat down on the bank. But fear of the seas' rolling and our coldness, would not suffer us there to remain. But we went up into the land and sat us down under a cedar tree, which the wind had thrown down, where we sat about an hour almost dead with cold. But now the storm was broken up, and the wind was calm, but the sea remained rough and fearful to us. My legs were much bruised, and so my head was; other hurt I had none, neither had I taken in much quantity of water, but my heart would not let me sit still any longer, but I would go to see if any more were gotten to the land in safety, especially hoping to have met with some of my own poor children; but I could find none, neither dead nor yet living. You condole with me my miseries who now begin to consider of my losses. Now came to my remembrance the time and manner how and when I last saw and left my children and friends. One was severed from me sitting on the rock at my feet, the other three in the pinnace. My little babe (ah, poor Peter), sitting in his sister Edith's arms, who to the utmost of her power sheltered him from the waters. My poor William standing close unto them, all three of them looking ruefully on me, on the rock, their very countenances calling unto me to help them, whom I could not go unto, neither could they come at me, neither would the merciless waves afford me space of time to use any means at all, either to help them or myself. Oh, I yet see their cheeks, poor silent lambs, plead pity and help at my hands. Then on the other side to consider the loss of my dear friends, with the spoiling and loss of all our goods and provisions; myself cast upon an unknown land in a wilderness, I knew not where nor how to get thence. Then it came to my mind how I had occasioned the death of my children, who caused them to leave their native land, who might have left them there, yea and might have sent some back again and cost me nothing; hese and such like thoughts do press down my heavy heart very much. But I must let this pass, and will proceed on in the relation of God's goodness unto me in that desolate island on which I was cast. I and my wife were almost naked both of us, and wet and cold even unto death. I found a snapsack cast on the shore in which I had a steel and flint and powder horn. Going further I found a drowned goat ; then I found a hat and my son William's coat, both of which I put on. My wife found one of her petticoats, which she put on. I found also two cheeses and some butter driven ashore. Thus the Lord sent us some clothes to put on, and food to sustain our new lives, which we had lately given unto us, and means also to make fire for in an hour I had some gunpowder, which to mine own (and since to other men's) admiration was dry. So taking a piece of my wife's neckcloth, which I dried in the sun, I struck a fire, and so dried and warmed our wet bodies, and then skinned the goat, and having found a small brass pot, we boiled some of her. Our drink was brackish water. Bread, we had none. There we remained until Monday following, when. about three of the clock in the after oon, in a boat that came that way, we went off that desolate island, which I named after my name, ' *Thacher's Woe*,' and the rock '*Avery, his fall*,' to the end that their fall and loss and mine own, might be had in perpetual remembrance. In the isle lieth buried the body of my cousin's eldest daughter, whom I found dead on the shore. On the Tuesday following, in the afternoon, we arrived at *Marblehead* "

A cradle coverlet, of scarlet broadcloth, originally trimmed with gold lace, but which souvenir hunters have entirely picked off, said to have been shipwrecked, is still in the possession of his descendants, and is held in great veneration.

In the Massachusetts Colonial Records, we find under date of September 3, 1635, the following :

"It is ordered that there shall be fforty markes given to Mr. Thacher out of the tresury towards his greate losses;" and under date of March 9, 1636-7, the following : " Mr. Anthony Thacher had granted him the small iland at the head of Cape Ann (vpon wch hee was pserved from shipwrack) as his pp inheritance."

In Governor Winthrop's Journal we find: " the General Court gave Mr. Thacher £26 13s. 4d. towards his losses, and divers good people gave him besides."

After his shipwreck, he probably remained in Marblehead for a time, as his son John was born there in 1638-9. From notes taken from the Plymouth Colonial Records, we find that a grant of land at Mattacheeset (now Yarmouth), was made to him and others January 7, 1638-9, and under date of March 5, of the same year, we find he was one of a committee for the division of land. We may therefore reasonably conclude that he had settled there, although his wife was still at Marblehead.

The house that Mr. Thacher built for a permanent residence, and in which he died, was situated on the north side of the town of Yarmouth, near the salt marsh. The exact spot was a little knoll about midway between the present residence of Mrs. James G. Hallett and Mr. Dustin Eldridge, at Yarmouth Port.

From the same records we find that Mr. Thacher took a prominent part in the affairs of the town and colony, and was employed in various public offices, and found faithful, for he was fined but once for not being at court, and it was remitted, being his first offence. In this he stood better than any of the other prominent men to whom our attention has been called. He represented the town of Yarmouth in the General Court at Plymouth in 1643, '44, '45, '46, '47, '51, '52, '54, '59, '63 and '65. The exact date of his death is not known, but it must have been sometime between June 30, 1667, and August 22 of the same year, as Mr. H. C. Thacher, of Boston, has a paper signed by him bearing the former date, and the inventory of his estate was taken at the latter date.

The exact spot of his burial is not known, but it was on his own land and not far from his house.

For his first wife he married (according to Farmer) Mary ——, who died at Salisbury, England, in 1634. Their children were:

⁴ William, born previous to 1620.

⁶ Mary, ⁸ Edith, ¹⁰ Peter.

These were all drowned in the shipwreck.

¹² Benjamin, who was left in Salisbury, and buried there September 4, 1639.

For a second wife he married Elizabeth Jones, six weeks previous to sailing for America. She survived him a few years. Their children were:

[14] John, born March 17, 1639; died May 8, 1713.

[16] Judah, born ———; died November 4, 1676.

[18] Bethian, born ———, married Jabez Howland, of Duxbury, and settled at Bristol, Rhode Island, after the conquest of Mount Hope, and had nine children. From this pair have descended a numerous family, who have scattered through the country.

Second Generation. [2-14] JOHN, the oldest son of *Anthony*, was born March 17, 1639. He was at an early age appointed an officer in the militia, and for more than twenty years served as one of the selectmen of the town of Yarmouth. In the year 1668, he was chosen a representative for the town to the General Court, and was elected to that station annually to the year 1683, except the year 1672. He was in the year 1681 chosen one of the council of war, and continued to serve several years, and was, for about five years, one of the assistants of the Governor. Immediately on the union of Plymouth colony with the province of Massachusetts Bay, under the charter of William and Mary, in 1692, Mr. Thacher was elected a member of the provincial council, and continued to serve in that capacity near twenty years. We also find from records that he held the rank of Colonel, and at his death was buried with military honors. He died at Yarmouth, May 8, 1713, aged seventy-five years.

Mr. Thacher was married November 6, 1661, to Rebecca Winslow, of Mansfield, daughter of the first Josiah Winslow, and niece of the first Governor Winslow. She was born July 16, 1642, and died July 15, 1683.

Family tradition furnishes a singular anecdote. On his return to Yarmouth with his bride and company, they stopped at the house of Colonel Gorham, at Barnstable. In the merry conversation with the newly married couple, an infant was introduced, about three weeks old, and it was observed to Mr. Thacher *that she was born on such a night,* he replied *that it was the very night he was married;* and, taking the child in his arms, presented it to his bride, saying, "Here, my dear, is a little lady born on the same night that we were married. I wish you would kiss it, as I intend to have her *for my second wife*. "I will, my dear," she replied, "to please you, but I hope it will be a long time before you have that pleasure!" so taking the babe she pressed it to her lips and gave it a kiss. This jesting prediction was eventually verified. Mr. Thacher's wife died, and the child, Lydia Gorham, arriving at mature age, actually became his wife, January 1, 1684, O. S. (January 11, N. S.)

Tradition also furnishes the following anecdote concerning the manner of obtaining the second wife. After the death of his first wife, John, while riding in Barnstable, saw a horse belonging to his son Peter, tied to a tree in front of Colonel Gorham's residence, and as a thoughtful parent is inclined, he went in to see what his son was doing, and found that he had advanced considerably in a suit with Miss Lydia, whom the father had prophetically declared would be his second wife; and whether it was on account of that prophecy, or that he had had his attention called to the girl before, he took Peter aside and offered him ten pounds, old tenor, and a yoke of black steers, if he would resign his claims.

Tradition does not say whether Peter was an obedient son and accepted the offer, or whether the father succeeded in spite of his rival.

No one would ever think after reading the three hundred and twenty-two lines that he wrote "Upon the great loss of his dear wife," Rebecca, dated August 30, six weeks after her death, that in four months he would have married again. She died June 2, 1744, in her eighty-third year. His children by his first wife, Rebecca Winslow, were:

[20] Peter, born May 20, 1665; died May 26, 1736.

[22] Josiah, born April 26, 1667; died May 12, 1702.

[24] Rebecca, born June 1, 1669; died ——. She married first James Sturgis; afterward Ebenezer Lewis.

[26] Bethiah, born July 10, 1671; died ——. She married James Paine, April 9, 1691, and had seven children.

[28] John, born January 28, 1674–5; died March 7, 1764.

[30] Elizabeth, born June 19, 1677, married Moses Hatch October 18, 1699, and had three children; died May 18, 1710.

[32] Hannah,[1] born August 19, 1679; died July 11, 1689.

[34] Mary,[1] born August 3, 1682; died September 7, 1682.

There was another child who died young.

His children by his second wife, Lydia Gorham, were:

[36] Lydia, born February 11, 1684–5, married Joseph Freeman of Harwich, and had six children; died September 3, 1724.

[38] Mary,[2] born February 5, 1686–7, married Colonel Shubael Gorham, of Barnstable; died June 28, 1778. Had six children.

[40] Desire, born December 24, 1688, married Josiah Crocker, of Barnstable; died May 6, 1723.

[42] Hannah,[2] born October 9, 1690, married Nathaniel Otis, of Colchester; died May 6, 1780.

[44] Mercy,[1] born July 23, 1692; died August 27, 1692.

[46] Judah, born August 20, 1693; died January 8, 1775.

[48] Mercy,[2] born December 28, 1695; died August 22, 1696.

[50] Ann, born May 7, 1697, married John Lothrop, removed to Tolland county, Connecticut; died March 13, 1756.

[52] Joseph, born July 11, 1699; died June 17, 1763.

[54] Benjamin, born June 25, 1702; died ——, 1768.

[56] Mercy,[3] born February 7, 1702–3; married 1724, James Harris, of Saybrook, Connecticut.

[58] Thomas, born April 2, 1705; died December 20, 1746, making twenty-one children in all, fourteen of whom married for the blessing of the Cape.

[2-16] JUDAH, the second son of *Anthony*, married Mary Thornton, daughter of Rev. Thomas Thornton. She died November 30, 1708, aged sixty-eight. He died November 4, 1676, at at Yarmouth. We find no traits of his character on record. His children were as follows:

[60] Elizabeth, born October 1667, married December 7, 1705, to Joshua Gee, afterwards to Rev. Peter Thacher, of Milton, in 1727.

[62] Thomas, born May 18, 1669; died ——.

[64] Mary, born March 17, 1671, married November 13, 1692. to Moses Draper, of Roxbury, afterward (August 17, 1704), to Joseph Grant, of Boston.

[66] Judah,[1] born 1673 (?); died October 6, 1676.

[68] Ann, born October 31, 1674; died unmarried.

[70] Judah,[2] born December 7, 1676; died 1705. A sailor and unmarried.

We have not been able to find any further account of the descendants of this family, but tradition says that [62] Thomas settled in Tolland County, Connecticut, but we have been unable to find any trace of him, and think it very doubtful.

Third Generation. [14-20] PETER, the eldest son of *Hon. John* and Rebecca Winslow, was born at Yarmouth April 26, 1665. He was a man of considerable note, and sustained many offices, as representative to the General Court, one of his majesty's Justices of the Peace, and first Justice of the Court of Common Pleas for the county of Barnstable. In September, 1729, he was appointed to have the care and government of the Indians, within the county of Barnstable, in all matters civil and criminal, authorized to appoint constables, and other proper officers among them. Mr. Thacher was for several years one of his majesty's honorable counsel. He was distinguished for benevolence, and revered for his piety to God, and for his integrity and uprightness in all his judicial proceedings. As a judge, he was said to be full of compassion, and when transgressors were before him, he appeared always to desire their reformation more than to inflict punishment. He manifested friendship and tenderness towards domestics, endeavoring constantly to impress on their minds the importance of an hereafter. As a Christian he was truly humble, esteeming others better than himself. He so discharged all trusts reposed in him, as to gain esteem, both in public and private life, and to leave behind him a universal good name.

He married Thankful Sturgis, of Barnstable, who died May 1, 1745, aged seventy. Their children were:

[82] Thankful, born January 13, 1693–4, married John Hallet, of Yarmouth, August 24, 1716; died February 9, 1768.

[84] Peter,[1] born December 11, 1695; died in infancy.

[86] Sarah, born February 2, 1708–9, married George Lewis, of Barnstable, September 12, 1737; died April 30, 1762.

[88] Temperance, born September 16, 1711, married Seth Crocker, of Barnstable, July 24, 1734; died July 11, 1736.

[90] Peter,[2] born August 24, 1712; died August 22, 1775.

[92] Hannah, born August 10, 1715; died June 14, 1748.

He died February 12, 1735–6, in the seventy-first year of his age, in full and unshaken hope of a better world.

[11-22] JOSIAH, second son of *Hon. John*, was born April 26, 1667, at Yarmouth. He held the office of deacon in the church. He married Mary Hedge, February 25, 1690–1, and died May 12, 1702. Their children were:

[94] Anthony, [96] Rebecca, married in 1716 to James Paddock, [98] Mary, married in 1719 to Joshua Sears, [100] Elisha, [102] Josiah, Jr.

[14-24] JOHN, the youngest son of *Hon. John*, by his first wife, was born at Yarmouth January 28, 1674–5, and resided in the east parish in the town of Barnstable. He sustained for about thirty years the office of Register of Deeds for the county, and was for many years Judge of the Court of Common Pleas, and colonel of a regiment of militia. He died March 17, 1764, at the great age of ninety years.

The following is inscribed on his tombstone on the south side of the east meeting house in Barnstable: "Here lies interred, the body of the Hon. John Thacher, who, after a long life of usefulness and faithfulness in several military offices, and of eminent exemplariness in the religion of Christ and in the hope of eternal life. Died March 17, 1764, in the ninetieth year of his age."

Colonel Thacher married Desire Sturgis Dimmock, November 10, 1698; she died March 29. 1744, aged eighty-three. Their children were:

[104] Abigail, born November 2, 1699, married Joseph Hallet, of Yarmouth, October 11, 1722; died ——.

[106] Elizabeth, born June 27. 1701, married Jonathan Davis; died ——.

[108] John, born June 25, 1703: died September, 1785.

[110] Lot, born May 23, 1705: died ——.

[112] Fear, born March 28, 1707, married Nathaniel Lewis; died November 14, 1758.

[114] Roland, born August 28, 1710; died February 18, 1775.

[14-46] JUDAH, son of *Hon. John*, was born August 20, 1693. He was a prominent merchant in the town of Yarmouth, and held many important offices in that town. He died June 8, 1775, and was the last surviving grandchild of *Anthony*. He married Sarah Crosby, June 4, 1724; she died October 20, 1771, aged sixty-nine years. Their children were:

[116] Joseph, born September 10, 1726; died December 24, 1771.

[118] David,[1] born May 30, 1728; died July 29, 1729.

[120] David,[2] born March 14, 1730; died November 9, 1801.

[122] Josiah, born February 2, 1732; died January 19. 1802.

[124] Judah, born January 29, 1734; died at Halifax, N. S.

[126] Sarah, born August 17, 1737, married Prince Hawes. Jr., of Yarmouth, October 17, 1765; second, Thomas Palmer, died ——.

[128] John, born August 25, 1739; died August 12. 1799.

[130] William, born March, 1743; died ——.

[14-52] JOSEPH, son of *Hon. John*, was born July 11, 1699, and was a popular character. Through his influence, principally, a company of forty, thirteen of whom were Indians, was raised, all except six or eight, in Yarmouth, his native town, to go on the Cape Breton expedition in 1745. A condition of their em-

barking in this bold enterprise was, that Mr. Thacher should be their captain. It is remarkable that, of the Indians, only three lived to return, two having been killed by the enemy, and eight, probably in consequence of a mode of living to which they had not been accustomed, dying of disease; and that the rest of the company, though exposed to great hardships, were providentially all spared to see their native places again, and to participate with their fellow-countrymen in the joy which pervaded the land, on the reduction of the strongest fortress of America. The following anecdote exhibits the unfeeling disposition of the American savage. Through the treacherous conduct of a certain Frenchman, a party of twenty provincial soldiers had been ambuscaded, nineteen of whom were killed. The Frenchman was taken, and at first was given up to the Indians, to be destroyed by them as they might see proper. Isaac Peck, a bloodthirsty Indian, began immediately to sharpen his knife, and, thinking it too good for the traitor to die at once, said he was going to begin with his fingers, and would cut off one joint first, then another, and so on, till he had separated all his bones from head to foot. He would probably have executed his purpose, had not the criminal been rescued from his hands.

One of Thacher's Indians, hired by Colonel Vaughan for a bottle of brandy, was the first of the provincials who entered the grand battery at Louisburgh. He crawled in at an embrasure and opened the gate, which Vaughan immediately entered, the enemy having withdrawn from this battery, though at the time the circumstance was not known.

Colonel Thacher married Ruth Hawes, February 29, 1727; she died May 3, 1772, aged sixty-two; he died June 17, 1763. Their children were:

[134] Desire, born July 5, 1730, married Rev. Grindall Rawson, of Yarmouth, January 25, 1756; died ——.

[136] Ebenezer, born February 17, 1733; died ——.

[138] Ruth, born September 11, 1736, married Ezekiel Webb, of Yarmouth, November 16, 1764, afterward Seth Whelden; died ——.

[141] Joseph, born May 19, 1744; died in the Revolutionary army.

[11-5] BENJAMIN, son of *Hon. John*, was born June 25, 1701, married Hannah Lumbert, of Barnstable, January 30, 1734. He removed to Harwich (now Brewster) and kept a tavern: also followed the sea for a time. He died in Harwich, 1768. Their children were:

[142] Benjamin, born February 11, 1737; died ——, 1775.

[144] Hannah, born ——, 1740; died April, 1813, aged 73.

[146] Sarah, born December 1, 1741, married Isaac Foster. 1764: died October 3, 1777.

[148] Lydia,[1] born May 9, 1743; died May 30.

[150] Lydia,[2] born September 10, 1744, married Samuel Foster. of Harwich, December 4, 1766: died in Dorchester in the autumn of 1829.

[152] Jonathan,[1] born April 18, 1746; died June ——, 1746.

[154] Jane, born July 30, 1747, married Shubael Cook, of Harwich, February 19, 1776; died in Dorchester.

[156] Jonathan,[2] born February 22, 1748; died ——.

[158] Temperance,[1] born April 9, 1750; died ——.

[160] Samuel, born January 17, 1752; died December 23, 1793.

Temperance,[2] born July 27, 1754, married William Ward, of Guilford or New London, Connecticut; died ——.

[11-5] THOMAS, youngest son of *Hon. John*, was born April 2, 1705, married Thankful Baxter, February 11, 1730–1. She survived him and married Captain Samuel Lumbert, of Barnstable, January 28, 1747–8. He was a mariner, and died at Annapolis December 20, 1746. Their children were:

Lydia, born August 31, 1736; died September 10, 1736.

Thomas, born August 13, 1740; died ——.

Elizabeth, born March 28. 1741–2, married Thomas Palmer, of Falmouth, May 26, 1763: died ——.

Thankful, born November 8, 1744, married Zachariah Allen. of Falmouth, December 30, 1765; died ——.

Fourth Generation. [20]-[90] PETER, JR., youngest son of *Peter*, was born August 24, 1712, married Anner Lewis, daughter of George Lewis, of Barnstable, October 24, 1734. He served some time in a military capacity, and we find him designated as *Lieutenant*. Their children were :

[196] Josiah, born July 25, 1735 ; died ——, 1799.

[198] Peter, born November 25, 1737 ; died September 21, 1802.

[200] Temperance, born February 22, 1739–40, married John Hedge, and had seven children ; died ——, 1805.

[202] Lewis[1] and Lewis[2], both died young.

[204] Thankful, born February 28, 1744–5 ; died March 5, 1764.

[206] Anner, born July 2, 1747 ; died August 9, 1748.

[208] Sarah, born June 5, 1749, married Isaac Gorham ; died January 28, 1808.

[210] Lewis,[3] born November 23, 1751 ; died November, 1778.

[212] George, born April 12, 1754 ; died April 6, 1824.

[214] Thomas, born January 20, 1757 ; died February 24, 1806–7.

[22]-[100] ELISHA, second son of *Deacon Josiah*, was born ——, married Phebe Lothrop, and their children were :

[216] Desire, born April 15, 1722, married William Taylor, June 2, 1743 ; died ——.

[218] Anthony,[1] born May 6, 1724 ; died ——.

[220] Phebe, born March 7, 1726 ; died ——.

[222] John, born September 1, 1730 ; died ——.

[224] Mary, born March 7, 1732, married Ebenezer Gorham, Jr., December 21, 1752 ; died ——.

[226] Elisha, born May 8, 1734 ; died ——.

[228] Lucretia, born April 20, 1737, married Joseph Davis, November 17, 1763.

[230] Samuel Sturgis, born November 4, 1741 ; died February 14, 1742.

[232] Anthony,[2] born June 28, 1744 ; died ——.

[22]-[102] JOSIAH, son of *Deacon Josiah*, was born at Yarmouth,

married Miss Burr, Bun or Bunce (probably Burr). In the parish records at Yarmouth, under date of August 20, 1732, we find he was dismissed to Norwalk or Norwich, Connecticut, but we have been unable to find any further trace of him, and should this come to the notice of any one knowing anything concerning him, they will confer a favor by communicating the same to George Winslow Thacher, of Yarmouth Port, Massachusetts.

²⁸⁻¹⁰⁸ JOHN, son of *Colonel John*, was born June 25, 1703. Being the oldest son he inherited and resided on the homestead at Barnstable. He was a mechanic and agriculturist, and sustained an unblemished reputation, being strictly religious in principle and practice. He died in September, 1785, aged eighty-one. He married Content Norton, of Chilmark, Martha's Vineyard, November 28, 1734. Their children were:

²¹⁶ Elizabeth, born February 29, 1735-6, married first, Hezekiah Jackson, of Plymouth, July 24, 1766, afterward Eleazer Stevens, died ——.

²¹⁸ Abigail, born March 20, 1738, married John Gray, November 24, 1763; died ——.

²⁵⁰ Content, born September 6, 1740; died ——.

²⁵² Rebecca, born August 7, 1742; died ——.

²⁵⁴ Desire, born July 18, 1745, married Benjamin Gorham, of Barnstable, October 15, 1775; died ——.

²⁵⁶ Jethro, born January 16, 1747; died June 28, 1826, at Lee.

²⁵⁸ Fear, born February 1, 1748, married John Goodwin, of Plymouth, December 11, 1777; died March 28, 1829.

²⁶⁰ John, born December 29, 1751; died July 4, 1833.

²⁶² James, born February 4, 1754; died May 26, 1844.

²⁶⁴ Mary, born March 16, 1757; died ——.

²⁶⁶ Samuel, born May 29, 1759; died ——, age 2 years 24 days.

²⁸⁻¹¹⁰ LOT, son of *Colonel John*, was born May 23, 1705, married Rebecca Kean, of Pembroke, September 27, 1730, was a mariner, and drowned December 15 or 16, 1732, crossing Cape Cod bay. Their children were:

[268] Mary, born May 29, 1731, married Jonathan Lothrop, December 12, 1751.

[270] Lot, born February 19, 1732-3; died ——.

[28-114] ROLAND, youngest son of *Colonel John*, was born August 28, 1710, at Barnstable. He was educated for the ministry, and graduated at Harvard College in 1733. He was the first pastor of the church and society at Wareham, where he was ordained in 1740, and was pastor for thirty-four years, and died greatly beloved and respected February 18, 1775, aged sixty-four. He married Abigail Crocker, and their children were:

[272] Martha F., born June 19, 1741, married Nathaniel Howland, of Barnstable, December 15, 1702; died at Lee October 10, 1825.

[274] Jerusha, born April 3, 1743, married John Gibbs, of Sandwich, January, 1763; died ——.

[276] Roland, born March 13, 1745; died March 29, 1813.

[278] Sylvia, born May 16, 1747, married Alvan Crocker, of Barnstable, November 30, 1768; died ——.

[280] Desire, born July 27, 1749, married David Nye, of Rochester, March 7, 1771; died January 4, 1815.

[282] Lucy, born May 27, 1751; died March 2, 1772.

[284] Abigail, born October 20, 1753; died February 13, 1775. His wife, Abigail, died October 31, 1753. He was afterwards married, September 16, 1754, to Mrs. Hannah Fearing (formerly Hannah Swift), who died June 29, 1774. Their children were:

[286] Hannah, born June 27, 1755, married her cousin, [256] Jethro Thatcher; died July 15, 1833, at Lee.

[288] Lot, born June 3, 1757; died March 4, 1833.

[290] Fear, born March 14, 1760, married Joshua Crocker, of Barnstable (moved to New Bedford); died September 8, 1833.

[292] Elizabeth, born September 23, 1762, married Israel Fearing, of Wareham. Moved to Newport, Rhode Island.

[294] John, born January 26, 1767; died at Montreal.

⁴⁶⁻¹¹⁶ JOSEPH, oldest son of *Judah*, was born September 10, 1726. He was a blacksmith, and resided in Yarmouth. He married Abigail Hawes, of that place, July 27, 1749. He died December 24, 1771: she died June 21, 1789. Their children were :

³⁰⁰ Solomon, born April 3, 1750; died October 25, 1798.

³⁰² Peleg, born November 22, 1751, married Mercy Mathews, September 21, 1780; died at Barnstable.

³⁰⁴ Ebenezer, born June 2, 1754; died April 1, 1831.

³⁰⁶ Lydia, born January 22, 1756, married Charles Hallet, of Yarmouth, June 5, 1777; died ———.

³⁰⁸ Isaac, born September 6, 1757; died unmarried.

³¹⁰ Joseph, born April 16, 1759: died ———.

³¹² Sarah, born May 10, 1761, married Joseph Vincent, December 10, 1789, and moved to Ashfield.

³¹⁴ Temperance, born December 22, 1762; died June 14, 1791.

³¹⁶ Daniel, born April 29, 1765; died young.

³¹⁸ Barnabas, born August 26, 1768; died September 26, 1836.

³²⁰ Ezekiel, born January 26, 1772; died ———, 1785.

⁴⁶⁻¹²⁰ DAVID, son of *Judah*, was born March 14, 1730, at Yarmouth, and inherited and lived on the place of his father's. He was a representative for thirty years, and senator for several years, in the General Court of Massachusetts, and was often employed on committees when maturity of judgment and experience, gained by a careful attention to the interests of the commonwealth were particularly required. This gentleman was distinguished by talents of the solid, judicious and useful, rather than the brilliant and showy kind. He held, during the great part of his life, various offices in town and country. He was one of the Committee of Safety, during the revolutionary war, and for fifteen years was one of the Judges of the Court of Common Pleas for the county of Barnstable. He was also a member of the conventions for forming and adopting the State and Federal Constitution. The place of his residence and death

was Yarmouth, county of Barnstable, where is a monumental stone consecrated "To the memory of the Hon. David Thacher, Esq., who having served his generation in many important public stations, with honor and fidelity, died November 9, 1801, aged seventy-two years. By a constant practice of the social virtues, he rendered himself greatly beloved and respected, in the various walks of domestic life. Reader, wouldst thou be honored in life and lamented in death, go and do likewise. Also, erected to the memory of Mrs. Abigail Thacher, widow of the Hon. David Thacher, Esq., who died April 25, 1803, aged seventy-six years. She was greatly esteemed as a Christian and a friend." They had six children, only one of whom, [332] David, jr., the youngest, arrived at maturity.

[46]-[122] JOSIAH, son of *Judah*, was born February 2, 1732–3, at Yarmouth. He was a tavern keeper for many years in that town, and held the office of deacon in the church. He married first Desire Crowell, of Yarmouth, February 22, 1759; she died February 27, 1788, aged fifty-eight years. For a second wife, he married Mary Hedge, of Yarmouth, January 1, 1789; she died January 15, 1811. He died January 19, 1802. There is a remarkable coincidence connected with this Josiah. We find that his uncle [22] Josiah, son of [14] John, held the office of deacon in the same church one hundred years before, and married a previous Mary Hedge. The first one died in 1702, this one in 1802. This coincidence has puzzled antiquarians, as they have confounded the two. The children by his first wife were:

[334] Mercy, born March 20, 1760, married Andrew Hedge, of Yarmouth, December 26, 1782.

[336] Judah, born July 2, 1762; lost at sea.

[338] James, born May 15, 1764; died November 28, 1832.

[340] Josiah, born July 1, 1766; died December 18, 1853.

[342] Desire, born February 6, 1769, married Daniel Taylor, of Yarmouth, December 7, 1793; she died February 25, 1825.

[344] Anne, born June 23, 1771, married Dr. John Duston, o Yarmouth, December 14, 1794; died ——.

[346] Edmund, born March 24, 1774; died ——.

[46]-[124] JOHN, son of *Judah*, born August 25, 1739, was town clerk of Yarmouth for a time. He married Hannah Mathews, October 18, 1766; she died April 26, 1832, aged eighty-four. He died August 12, 1799. Their children were:

[348] Rebecca, born November 23, 1767, married William Bray, second, December 1, 1788; died June 30, 1795.

[350] John, born ——, 1769; died March 7, 1820.

[352] Hannah, born August 17, 1771, married Sylvanus Kelly, of Yarmouth, February 3, 1791; died October 8, 1849.

[354] Isaiah, born November 6, 1773, sailed from Cape Ann, September 21, 1798; supposed to have been lost in a gale on the 25th.

[356] Job, born December 30, 1776; died at sea 1802.

[358] Elkinah, born January 18, 1779; died at sea 1802.

[360] Sally, born April 19, 1782; died November 17, 1862.

[362] Elizabeth,[1] born April 19, 1782; died May 29, 1783.

[364] Isaac, born September 25, 1784; died at sea 1801.

[366] Mathews, born June 8, 1788; died October 25, 1868.

[368] Elizabeth,[2] born June 8, 1788, married Ebenezer Mathews, of Yarmouth, January 24, 1811; died March 5, 1862.

[46]-[130] WILLIAM, youngest son of *Judah*, was born at Yarmouth March 30, 1743, moved to South Dartmouth, Massachusetts, about 1803. He was a house and ship carpenter, and a man of considerable genius, introducing many improvements in salt works and wind mills. He held the office of deacon in the church. He married Thankful Hedge, who died April 7, 1823; he died May 24, 1829. Their children were:

[370] Mehitable,[1] born October 25, 1768; died ——.

[372] Laban, born September 9, 1772; died March 3, 1833.

[374] Molly G., born June 10, 1775; married Benjamin Kelly, of Yarmouth, September 27, 1792; died April 22, 1799.

[376] Thankful, born July 31, 1780, married Captain Ebenezer Hawes, September, 1799.

[378] Judah, born August 28, 1784; died ——.

[380] William, born August 28, 1784; died December 3, 1853.

[382] Mehitable,[2] born April 1, 1787, married Benjamin Kelly, January 22, 1804; died December 16, 1841.

[384] Gorham, born April 25, 1790; died ——.

[52-140] JOSEPH, son of *Colonel Joseph*, was born May 19, 1744, at Yarmouth, and died in the revolutionary army. He married Susannah Whelden, of Yarmouth. Their children were:

[386] Polly, born October 28, 1766, married Abiel Lovejoy, of Vassalboro', November 8, 1788; died ——.

[388] Joseph, born February 8, 1769; died August 30, 1790.

[390] Ruth Hawes, born August 5, 1771, married Philip Baker, September 24, 1793; died ——.

[392] Ebenezer, born January 23, 1774; drowned in Saco River, Maine, aged 13.

[394] Susannah, born June 19, 1776; married [338] James Thacher, of Yarmouth.

[396] Jonathan ——.

[54-142] BENJAMIN, son of *Benjamin*, was born February 11, 1737–8, lived in Harwich (now Brewster), and was a mariner. Married Desire Freeman, of Harwich, in 1756. Their children were:

[398] Desire, [400] Benjamin.

[54-160] SAMUEL, son of *Benjamin*, was born January 17, 1752, married Lucy Fessenden, of Harwich, was a man of superior education, and a master mariner; died at sea December 23, 1793. He had one child, [402] Sarah, born April 23, 1781, married Isaac Foster, of Harwich, September 7, 1797; she died February 28, 1861.

Fifth Generation. [90-196] JOSIAH, son of *Lieutenant Peter*, was an officer in the Revolutionary army, married Elizabeth Hamblin June 3, 1763; had two sons who died young. She died May 10, 1773, aged thirty-five. He married for a second wife, Elizabeth Lothrop, of Kingston, November 12, 1776. He died at Kingston, 1799.

[90-198] PETER, son of *Lieutenant Peter*, married Betty Howes, January 17, 1765. She died July 28, 1820. He died at Yarmouth September 21, 1822. Their children were:

[401] Samuel, born January 27, 1756; died July 6, 1756.

[406] Thankful, born March 26, 1768; married Isaac Hedge, November 7, 1793.

[408] James, born May 22, 1771, married Achsah Handy, and had [806] Betsey H., [808] Sophia, who married William Lovejoy, [810] Almira, who married David Towne. He died in Vassalboro', Maine.

[410] Peter,[1] born May 19, 1772; died March 19, 1773.

[412] Peter,[2] born June 17, 1774, married first Lydia Marston, of Barnstable, afterward Anna Davis, of Barnstable; died September 20, 1853.

[414] Henry,[1] born May 31, 1775; died ———, 1775.

[416] Henry,[2] born February 13, 1777; died ———, 1777.

[418] Henry,[3] born July 4, 1778; died July 27, 1833.

[420] Betsey Howes, born July 11, 1779; died July 16, 1780.

[422] Lewis, born September 11, 1781; died ———.

[90-212] GEORGE, son of *Lieutenant Peter*, was born at Yarmouth April 12, 1754, and graduated at Harvard College in 1776.

"He was at college cotemporary with King, Gore, Sewell, Dawes, and other distinguished men, who, through life, retained for him sentiments of affection and attachment. Having prepared himself for the profession of law, he began the practice of it in Biddeford, Maine, and was for many years a practitioner. Before the adoption of the federal constitution, he was chosen by the members of the legislature, a delegate to congress, and afterwards was successfully elected by the people a member of that honorable body until 1801, when he resigned his seat, and accepted the appointment of an associate justice of the Supreme Judicial Court of Massachusetts, where he remained for more than twenty years. While in congress Judge Thacher was, by no means, an undistinguished member. The debates of that period will show that he took an active part in all the important concerns of the time, and his speeches will be found to contain, in the midst of frequent irony and sometimes sharp satire, much useful information and sound argument. His opponents often cowered under the lashes of wit and ridicule which he bestowed upon what he thought was hollow pretence of patriotism; but such was the universal opinion of the goodness of his heart and the honesty of his views, that no one felt any anger or resentment except in one* memorable instance, in which his independent and manly conduct did more toward bringing the custom of dueling into contempt, than anything which had occurred in congress before or since. He refused to fight, and, instead of sinking in the opinion even of fighting men, overwhelmed his antagonist with confusion. On the bench of the Supreme Court, Judge Thacher was a faithful and upright public servant. His mind was well stored with legal principles, and his strong memory enabled him to apply them to the question which occurred, with great facility. His associates upon the bench have often been heard to say, that in their consultation upon cases argued, his discriminating power, sound technical knowledge, and recollection of old cases not reported, have been invaluable to them. His integrity, independence, impartiality and firmness, have been surpassed by none who have adorned the seat

---

* It is said that when in Congress, a bill was reported in respect to the eagle to be imprinted on the American coin. He opposed it, saying " that the eagle was a royal bird, not suitable for our democracy, but the figure of a goose would be very proper to be stamped on the dollar, in which case the goslings would be right for the dimes."

For this speech he was challenged by the reporter of the bill, and he replied to the second, who brought the challenge, " that he would write a note consulti .g Mrs. Thacher on the subject—in the meantime the challenger might mark his size on a wall and fire at it with a pistol, and if he hit it, he would acknowledge that he was shot." This ended the matter.

of justice. But it is in private life, among his friends and in his family, that we are to look for those virtues or blemishes which exhibit the real features of moral beauty or deformity that make up the character of man. His heart was most disinterestedly benevolent and kind; all human beings were his friends and brothers. He either could not see faults, or he would not acknowledge them. Even the poor criminals at the box, had sometimes more of his compassion than suited the stern demand of justice. He had a vein of wit and humor which irresistibly propelled him to put into ludicrous shapes the arguments and opinions of those with whom he entered into the war of words; but his heart never took side in the struggle, and the first appearance of wounded feelings would blunt his weapons and make him give the field to his adversary. In his domestic relations, he had no faults, unless an excess of kindness and indulgence be one. He lived a life of patriarchal simplicity. Surrounded by his sons and daughters and their children, and sharing the government of his family upon equal terms, with a most exemplary and excellent wife, his humble dwelling was the abode of peace, love and benevolence. It was also the scene of the most unlimited frugal hospitality, where every human face was received with welcome. Judge Thacher was a man of great and various reading, and was particularly versed in the theological and polemic controversies. This was frequently the subject of his conversation and writings, and his particular friends knew that he was a sincere believer in the great doctrines of Christianity—in immortality brought to light by Jesus Christ—in a future state of retribution. He laughed at the disputes which prevail in the Christian church, and perhaps had some peculiar notions; but he was a Christian. It is enough to say that he was a member of a christian church: for no particle of hypocrisy entered into his composition. He was a practical *Christian*, and his whole life would bear to be tested by the gospel, as much as the life of any who have doubted his faith. His life has been a happy one; he wanted nothing but comfort, friends and family love, and he was rich in all these. He never aimed at accumulating property. He had lived for others more than for himself. He died in the humble cottage endeared to him by forty years' familiarity, where everything was the work of his own hands, with the wife of his youth to soothe his last moments, and his numerous children to receive his parting blessing. He has departed in peace with the world, leaving no enemy behind him, and many friends who dwell upon his memory with affection and delight. Eccentricities he had, it is true; but they were innocent, sportive and amusing. No one who had occasion to consult his heart, ever found that erring or trifling; and it may be added, that no man lives, who, with such narrow means, has bestowed more upon the unfortunate."

If on any subject Judge Thacher devoted himself with enthusiastic ardor, it was that of tracing the genealogy of his ancestry, from the earliest period of their emigration to this country. No man could delight more in the contemplation of the characters and peculiar circumstances of his progenitors. He had with the most indefatigable industry collected materials and formed a correct genealogical tree, with all its collateral expanding branches from the original stock, the first Anthony Thacher, having acquired a perfect knowledge of every family and every individual bearing the name, down to the year 1816, and we have availed ourselves of his collection in composing the present sketches. He was married July 20, 1784, to Sarah Savage, of Weston, Massachusetts, and their children were:

⁴²⁴ Samuel P., born April, 1785; died November 5, 1842, at Mobile.

⁴²⁶ Sally B., born 1787, married Joseph Adams, of Sudbury; died 1827.

⁴²⁸ George, born September, 1790; died 1857, at Westford, Me.

⁴³⁰ Lucy S., born 1792, married October 16, 1815, to Abner Sawyer, of Saco, Maine; died August, 1820.

⁴³² Henry S., born June 25, 1794; died ——.

⁴³¹ Lewis, born January 16, 1796; died at Babylon, L. I., 1830.

[436] Anna L., born 1797, married September 20, 1821, to Chas. T. Savage.

[438] Josiah, born 1800; died at Biddeford, 1836.

[440] Nancy B.

[442] Elizabeth J., married August, 1827, to John T. Balch.

Judge Thacher died April 6, 1824, aged seventy years, wanting six days.

[90_214] THOMAS, son of *Lieutenant Peter*, was a man of great usefulness in his native town of Yarmouth, was Colonel of a military regiment, and employed in various public services, in which he acquitted himself with fidelity and honor. He married Mary Churchill, of Barnstable. She died November 23, 1841, aged eighty-four. He died February 24, 1806. Their children were:

[444] Anner Lewis, born Dec. 2, 1787; died February 26, 1851.

[446] Polly C., born April 29, 1791; died April 25, 1826.

[448] Thomas,[1] born December 27, 1793; died May 11, 1795.

[450] Thomas,[2] born July 25, 1795; died ——.

[452] George C., born December 30, 1796; died October, 1856.

[454] Sally, born May 13, 1800; died July 16, 1802.

[100_226] ANTHONY, son of *Elisha*, married Elizabeth Taylor, of Barnstable, where he resided. She survived him, and died August 6, 1818. Their children were:

[456] Elisha, who married and moved to Virginia.

[458] Phebe, married Edward Loring and had fourteen children.

[460] Betsey, married John Hinckley, and had six children.

[101_228] ELISHA, son of *Elisha*, married Abigail Webb, of Braintree, afterward to Mary Grove of Maryland, and had a daughter, [462] Abigail W., who married —— Hall, and died, leaving no children.

[103_230] JETHRO, son of *John*, married his cousin, [296] Hannah

Thatcher, daughter of Rev. [42] *Roland*, July 9, 1776, and settled in Barnstable. Their children were:

[464] Lucy, born December 29, 1777, married Ebenezer Swift, February 18, 1796; died July 15, 1811, aged thirty-three years.

[466] Jonathan, born April 21, 1780; killed by the kick of a horse he was attempting to drive home from Alford, Massachusetts, December 14, 1807. [A pillar by the road side still marks the spot where he came to his tragical end.]

[468] Martha, born June 23, 1783; died August 4, 1806, while on a visit to her sister in Barnstable.

[470] Nancy, born October 8, 1785; died January 7, 1872, at the residence of her niece, Mrs. Gibbs, at King's Ferry, Cayuga county, New York, aged eighty-six.

[472] Roland, born May 13, 1788; died October 4, 1813.

[474] Hannah, born September 24, 1790, married in 1815, James Wakefield, of Lee, Massachusetts; died November 10, 1850.

[476] Sophia, born October 30, 1792, married Leonard Olmstead; died at Elmira, New York.

"A short time after the marriage of their eldest daughter, Jethro and Hannah Thatcher becoming dissatisfied with the Unitarian influence which pervaded in the community and had taken possession of the church where they worshipped, removed with their family to Lee, Mass., that they might enjoy the pastoral ministrations of the Rev. Dr. Hyde. There they established themselves on a farm, and they were active, earnest workers, helping to build up a Christian community in that young town." Jethro died at Lee, June 28, 1826.

[108-216] JOHN, son of *John*, appears to have been a popular character, judging from the number of offices which he held. He was Deputy Marshall and High Sheriff, besides holding other minor offices. The following account of him was furnished by his son, the late Samuel Thacher, of Yarmouth, a short time before his death :

"The first United States mail between Boston and Barnstable, commenced running in 1792, when John Thacher, of Barnstable, contracted with the government to perform the service, and made the first trip October first, of that year. Timothy Pickering, of Pennsylvania (not the Massachusetts Pickering). was Postmaster General, and Jonathan Hastings, Postmaster at Boston. The arrangement was made through the influence of Shearjashub Bourne, the then member of Congress for this District. The post rider used to start on horseback from Barnstable, and arriving at Plymouth in the evening, stop in that town over night. The next night he arrived in Boston, at the sign of the Lion, on Washington street, and delivered his mail to the postmaster. Starting from Boston Thursday morning, he arrived at Barnstable on Friday night. The mail was easily carried in one side of a pair of saddle-bags. The other side was devoted to packages. For this service the contractor was paid one dollar per day while in actual service. This sum looks pretty niggardly beside the amounts now paid for government service, but small as it was, its was severely censured then for its extravagance. Moses Hallett, who seems to have been a champion in his day of reform and retrenchment, thought the sum paid exorbitant, and predicted that the government would go to ruin. But his opposition was unavailing, and it is safe to assert that a less sum never was paid for this service."

He died July 4, 1833. He married first Hannah Bourne, of Sandwich, September 26, 1773; she died January 1, 1785, aged twenty-nine. Their children were:

[178] Samuel, born October 11, 1789; died 1870.

[180] John, born May 1, 1783; died June 17, 1827. For a second wife he married Remembrance Freeman, of Sandwich, July 28, 1785. She died April 26, 1795. Their children were:

[182] Benj., born May 20, 1786; died in Canada June 10, 1832.
[184] James, born January 28, 1789; drowned September 1, 1821.
[186] Hannah B., born January 2, 1792; died ——.
[188] Freeman, born November 29, 1794; died ——.

For a third wife, he married Polly Simmons, September 23,

1795; she died April 28, 1814. For a fourth wife he married Sabria Hinckley, of Barnstable, September 5, 1814; she died 1834.

[108-262] JAMES, son of *John*, was born February 4, 1754, married Susannah Hayward, of Bridgewater. He was a public spirited and distinguished citizen, and died May 24, 1844, aged ninety years. We quote from his memoirs concerning himself, written July, 1834, a part of which we consider particularly applicable to the present times.

"Having devoted a few years to the study of medicine, under the direction of my patron, Dr. Abner Hersey, of Barnstable, and having imbibed a good share of the pure principles of the whigs and patriots of the day, I resolved to test my courage in the great 'rebellion' of 1775. In this service I continued seven years and a half, and participated in the glorious consummation of Independence. Since that period about half a century has been devoted to the practice of medicine, no less laborious both to body and mind than that of my military career. It is through the favor of the power from on high that I am yet among the living, a monument of a hoary head, crowned with innumerable, undeserved blessings. While yet I live, let me not live in vain. But God forbid that I should ever totter under the painful apprehension of witnessing my country's ruin. I have a recollection of days fraught with wondrous things and wondrous results; but the things of the present day are no less wondrous. I have seen our precious liberties and freedom wrested from the hands of the oppressors, by the immense sacrifice of lives, of treasure, of perils, and of sufferings. How many have I seen, at the hour of death, exclaiming—'I die for my country!' I see now the fair heritage of our fathers in imminent danger of being sacrificed at the shrine of a *reckless, sordid spirit of party interest*. I have seen public offices courting competent men to fill them, and I have seen them filled with men who, with a religious conscientiousness acquitted themselves of duty. But this seems already to be antiquated morality, for I now see unworthy, incompetent

men, seeking and laying claim to public offices as a reward for
desecration and unfaithfulness.   My fellow citizens, I have seen
the *days that tried men's souls.*   I claim the privilege of age to
forewarn you, that unless you view your elective franchise in a
light more precious than heretofore, ere long you will have no
office to bestow; all will be anarchy and confusion, ruin and
despair.   Oh ! how great would be my consolation, could my
benediction avail for the amelioration of my beloved country's
welfare."

He was the first Librarian of the Plymouth Historical Society,
and was the author of several works during his life.   Among
them were, a "Military Journal, "New Dispensary," "On
Hydrophobia," "Modern Practice of Physic," "American Or-
chardist," 1822, "American Medical Biography," 2 vols., 1828,
"On Management of Bees," 1831, "On Demonology, Ghosts,"
&c., 1831, "History of Plymouth," 1832, and sundry communi-
cations to societies and periodicals.   His children were:

[490] Betsey, who married Mr. Elliot, of Georgia, and had Catharine and Jane.   She afterwards married Michael Hodge, of
Newburyport, and had James T. Hodge.

[492] Susan, married Captain William Bartlett, of Plymouth, and
had children, among whom is John Bartlett, of Boston.

[491] James Hersey, died young.

[410-270] LOT, son of *Lot*, married Martha Taylor, of Bristol,
October 23, 1758, and had [496] Lot, born ——, died at Charleston,
South Carolina, unmarried.   [398] Rebecca.

[114-276] *Deacon* ROLAND, son of *Rev. Roland*, married June
28, 1773, Elizabeth Nye, of Rochester, Mass.   He removed
from Wareham to Lee, Berks county, and was among the first
settlers of that town.   Their children were:

[500] Timothy, born February 15, 1774; died at Lee, October
30, 1833.

[502] Lucy, born August 17, 1775, married September 2, 1792,
to Nathan Tobey of Sandwich; died April 26, 1802.

[504] Abigail, born May 27, 1777, married Joshua Briggs; died December 13, 1846.

[506] Roland, born February 6, 1779; died May 5, 1809.

[508] Stephen, born March 6, 1781, still living (May 1, 1872) at Saratoga Springs, in his ninety-second year.

[510] Adah, born December 12, 1783, married John Ells, of Lenox, June 18, 1804; died March 23, 1812.

[512] Desire, born March 2, 1786; died September 20, 1786.

[116-238] LOT, son of *Rev. Roland*, by his second wife, was born at Wareham, June 3, 1757, married Abigail Fearing, of Wareham, and removed to Rochester, Massachusetts, where he died March 4, 1833. Their children were:

[516] Sarah, or Sally,[1] born August 6, 1779, married Barnabas Waterman, of Hudson, New York; died September 6, 1809.

[518] David, born August 28, 1781; died August 22, 1849.

[520] Harrison, born December 24, 1783, married and lived in Maine, but had no children; died July 19, 1853.

[522] Charles Fearing, born May 4, 1786; died ——.

[524] Lewis, born September 26, 1788; died February 9, 1811.

[526] Peter, born August 21, 1790; still living at Boston.

[528] Allen, born July 17, 1793; still living at Middleboro'.

[530] Israel Fearing, born November 20, 1795; still living at Middleboro'.

[532] Abigail F., born April 1, 1798, married Nathaniel Sears, of Rochester.

[534] John, born May 1, 1800; died in Middleboro', 1872, unmarried.

[536] George, born June 27, 1802; died January 13, 1803.

His wife, Abigail, died March 19, 1803. He afterwards married Mrs. Huldah Miller, who died July 8, 1836, and had

[538] Albert, born July 4, 1805; died Nov. 5, 1846, unmarried.

[540] Sally,[2] born April 6, 1809; died March 22, 1811.

[114-294] JOHN, youngest son of *Rev. Roland*, was born January

26, 1767, married Parna Robinson, of Rainham, and removed to Lee, Mass. She died at Buffalo, N. Y. Their children were: [542] Lucy, [544] Luther Robinson, [546] Sylvia, [548] Hannah, [550] Thomas, [552] Emily, [554] Harriet. He died at Montreal, but was buried in Lee. [We have been unable to get any definite records of this family though some of them married and have children.]

[115.300] SOLOMON, son of *Joseph,* married Susannah Crosby, December 5, 1774. She died September, 1808, aged fifty-four. He died at Yarmouth, October 25, 1798. Their children were:

[556] Abigail, born October 28, 1775, married William Hallet, of Yarmouth, December 27, 1799; died ——.

[558] Lydia,[1] born August 21, 1777; died November 15, 1777.

[560] Phebe, born November 10, 1778, married Capt. Hezekiah Gorham, of Yarmouth, February 4, 1800; died ——, 1859.

[562] Lydia,[2] born June 1, 1781, married John Hallet, of Yarmouth, November 21, 1799; died ——.

[564] Anner, born August 29, 1783, married Bangs Hallet, of Yarmouth, December 7, 1803; died ——.

[566] Samuel, born October 4, 1786; died October, 1871.

[568] Solomon, born September 1, 1790; died September 30, 1811.

[570] Susannah,[1] born August 6, 1792; died October 18, 1793.

[572] Susannah,[2] born December 25, 1793; died ——.

[574] Benjamin, born September 14, 1796; died April 9, 1860.

[116.301] EBENEZER, son of *Joseph,* married Tamsen Taylor, June 30, 1785; she died March 20, 1828. He died at Yarmouth April 1, 1831. Their children were:

[576] Peleg, born July 15, 1787; died ——.

[578] Lothrop T., born June 24, 1790; died ——.

[580] Ruth, born December 8, 1792; died May 22, 1866.

[582] Lucy, born April 29, 1795, married Jonathan Hallet, jr., of Yarmouth, July 29, 1813; died January 11, 1839.

[584] Temperance,[1] born July 16, 1797; died August, 1799.

[586] Temperance,[2] born October 5, 1800, married Ebenezer Tay-

lor, jr., of Yarmouth, February 22, 1826; died August 14, 1867, at Roxbury.

[588] Ebenezer, born February 6, 1803; died at Havana, 1821.

[590] Charles, born June 30, 1807, married [694] Hannah Thacher, and resides in Yarmouth. She died in 1871.

[116-310] JOSEPH, son of *Joseph*, was a master mariner, and lived at Yarmouth. He married Abigail Gorham. She died September 22, 1821, aged sixty-two. Their children were:

[592] Daniel, born November 8, 1784; died August, 1788.

[594] Betsey,[1] born January 16, 1787; died ——, 1798.

[596] Joseph, born July 4, 1789; died ——.

[598] Samuel G., born May 20, 1792, married and lived in South Hanson, Massachusetts.

[600] Daniel, born July 9, 1793.

[602] Freeman, born June 1, 1796; died at sea previous to March 1, 1818.

[604] Nabby, born July 1, 1798, married first Captain Leonard Small, of Yarmouth, September 1822, married second, Henry Moore, of New York.

[606] Betsy,[2] born July 16, 1802, married Rev. —— Currier.

[116-318] BARNABAS, son of *Joseph*, married Mary Howes, of Yarmouth, April 18, 1793; she died August 11, 1838. He died September 26, 1832. Their children were:

[608] Ezekiel, born May 1, 1794.

[610] George, born April 2, 1796, married and died in Boston, and had children, among whom was William S. Thacher.

Sarah, born March 10, 1798.

[612] Barnabas, born April 4, 1800; died ——.

[614] Edward, born January 25, 1802; died ——, 1871.

[616] Olive, born December 14, 1803.

[618] Anner, born March 14, 1806.

[620] Isaac, born July 7, 1808; still living in Boston.

[622] Mary, born ——.

[120-332] DAVID, Jr., son of *David*, received a college education and was for many years a leading man in the town of Yarmouth. On account of better opportunities for business, he removed to Dartmouth, where he built the first salt works. He failed in business on account of the embargo of 1812, and afterwards removed to Egg Harbor, New Jersey, and died in that State in reduced circumstances. He was a man of superior education, and was noted for his courteous and urbane manners. He married for his first wife Sarah Gray, of Yarmouth, July 4, 1786; she died July 21, 1793. Their children were:

Sally ——, [624] Lothrop Russell, born May 22, 1788.

David,[1] born ——; died August 16, 1793, an infant.

For a second wife married Eunice W. Noble, June 12, 1796. Their children were:

[626] David,[2] born April 28, 1797.

[628] Oliver N., born August 9, 1798.

[630] Henry, born July 17, 1799.

[632] Fredrick, born July 16, 1800.

[634] Arthur, born ——, 1801.

[636] Abigail, born December 29, 1802.

[638] Lucy W., born ——.

[640] Alfred, [642] Cyrus, [644] Eunice Noble, [646] Charles, [648] Martha R.

[122-338] JAMES, son of *Josiah*, married [398] Susannah Thacher, February 15, 1795; she died September 28, 1823, aged forty-seven. He died November 28, 1832. Their children were:

[650] Polly, born July 25, 1796, married William Hall, of Yarmouth, September 11, 1817.

[652] Nancy,[1] born September 19, 1798; died October 19, 1804.

[654] Eunice, born August 10, 1800; died November 9, 1823.

[656] Joseph, born June 25, 1802; died at sea 1827.

[658] James, born June 10, 1804; lost at sea 1827.

[660] Nancy,[2] born April 10, 1806, married Enoch Brown, of Pawtucket.

[662] Judah, born June 29, 1808; sailed for the West Indies in 1832, and was never afterwards heard from.

[664] Susan, born September 26, 1810, married Captain Ansel Mathews, of Yarmouth, 1833.

[665] Fredrick, born November 25, 1812; died October 6, 1849, at Brooklyn, where his widow, Hannah, still resides. Had Henry, who died in 1868; Fredrick, who was drowned young; Josephine, married in 1870.

[668]. Alfred, born July 18, 1816, married Susan Baker, and resides in Illinois. Had Edmund and Ellen.

[670] Prentiss, born October 9, 1818, married Catharine Harris and resided in Pawtucket and New York.

[672] Matilda, born February 17, 1823; died April 8, 1823.

He married for a second wife, Susannah Hall, of Yarmouth, July, 1828; she died September 2, 1862, aged eighty-eight.

[122-310] JOSIAH, son of *Josiah*, married Lydia Mathews, of Yarmouth, June 16, 1791; she died October 14, 1836. He died December 18, 1853. Their children were:

[674] Harriet, born March 14, 1792; married David Ryder, of Yarmouth, 1813.

[676] Desire, born September 23, 1793, married Josiah Nickerson in 1817.

[678] Judah, born June 11, 1795; died May 13, 1797.

[680] Paddock, born June 25, 1797; died December 25, 1867.

[682] Josiah, born July 6, 1799; died ——, 1840.

[684] Lydia Hedge, born August 7, 1801; died January, 1820.

[686] Mary Grey, born August 5, 1804, married Francis Albert Jerrot, of France.

[688] Fanny, born June 11, 1806, married Ophis Josselyn, of Chatham, Mass., December 20, 1836.

[690] Russell, born September 30, 1809; lost at sea June 7, 1823.

[692] Allen, born July 29, 1811; died August 15, 1812.

[694] Hannah, born August 13, 1813, married [590] Chas. Thacher.

[122-315] EDMUND, son of *Josiah*, married Polly Bassett, of Yarmoth, July 24, 1799, removed to Vassalboro', Maine, and had

[696] Jonathan, born February 10, 1800.

[698] Betsey, born December 30, 1801.

[700] Mary Ann, born at Vassalboro'.

[128-350] JOHN, son of *John*, married Deborah Sears, of Yarmouth, February 23, 1792. He moved to South Dartmouth, 1805. He and his two sons, [706] Sears and [711] John sailed from Dartmouth March 7, 1820, and were supposed to have been lost that night, making five sons and two grandsons of [128] John, lost at sea. Their children were:

[702] Lavinia, born October 2, 1792; still living.

[704] Sears, born October 3, 1797; drowned as above.

[706] Rebecca, born October 3, 1797; died April 1, 1850.

[708] Isaiah, born September 26, 1799; died January 17, 1801.

[710] Serena, born June 28, 1802, married Ebenezer Alden, and resides in Fair Haven, Massachusetts.

[712] Sarah, born October 7, 1803, married —— Parker, of New Bedford.

[714] John, born November 26, 1804; lost at sea as above.

[716] Job, born January 1, 1807; died January 3, 1807.

[718] Isaac, born January 1, 1807; died January 18.

[720] Deborah, born July 14, 1808; living in 1870.

[722] Charlotte, born April 3, 1812; died February 12, 1813.

[128-366] MATHEWS, son of *John*, married Betsey Crocker, of Tiverton. She died July 6, 1862, aged seventy. He resided at Dartmouth most of his life, but died at Centerville October 25, 1868, being the last lineal descendant of Antony, in the fifth generation. Their children were:

[724] Isaiah Crocker, born July 2, 1815; still living.

[726] Rodolphus W., born July 3, 1817; died young.

[728] Ophelia C., born ——, 1819, married Captain Peter Butler.

[730] Clarissa Dexter, born 1821, married Rev. George Dunham.

[732] Harriet Dunbar, born 1823, married Capt. Hillman Crosby.

[734] Betsey, born December 26, 1825; still living.

[736] Henry Martin, born 1827, married and had children.

[738] John, born 1832, married Achsah Dexter, and had a son, Roland.

[130_372] LABAN, son of *William*, was a ship builder in Yarmouth. In 1805, he removed to the southern part of the town of Dartmouth, and the village which grew up around his ship yard was called Padan-aram, because Laban settled there. He afterward removed to New York, and engaged in business in that city, where he died of cholera March 3, 1833. He married Sally Davis, of Barnstable, February 2, 1792; she died November 3, 1833, in New Bedford. Their children were:

[740] Davis, born August 4, 1793.

[742] Watson, born June 23, 1795; was a merchant in Charleston, South Carolina; died about 1818.

[744] Laban, jr., born August 1, 1797; died January 18, 1839.

[746] Edward, died October, 1799, an infant.

[748] Stephen, born October 31, 1800.

[750] Isaac, born July 7, 1802; still living.

[752] Warren O., born July 7, 1804; still living.

[754] Sally D., born October 2, 1812; died an infant.

[756] Otis, born July 13, 1815; drowned July 18, 1820.

[130_378] JUDAH, son of *William*, married first Polly Howland, and resided at South Dartmouth. Their children were:

[760] Sally, married Edward S. Loring, of Booth Bay, Maine.

[762] Parmelia, died ——, aged eight years.

[764] Mary, married Amasa T. Smith, of Barnstable, now of Provincetown.

For a second wife he married Rebecca R. Custis, of Yarmouth, a cousin of the first husband of Martha Washington. They had one child, [766] Judah, lost at sea, aged about fifteen.

[130_380] WILLIAM, son of *William*, was a ship builder at Chatham, Massachusetts, where he died December 3, 1850. He married Hannah Howland; she died July 17, 1856, aged seventy-six. Their children were:

[768] Hetta, born August 17, 1806, married in Dartmouth, where she died March 25, 1867.

[770] Anthony, born December 4, 1807.

[772] Almira, born May 16, 1810, married Captain Edmund N. Doane, of Chatham.

[774] Benjamin Howland, born July 17, 1812; died at Pensacola, September 25, 1839.

[776] Polly, born September 19, 1814, married Sparrow Nickerson. Resides in Chicago.

[778] Lucretia, born March 3, 1817, married Lendol N. Doane; died July 11, 1847.

[780] William, born July 13, 1820.

[782] John, born March 17, 1823; died at sea October 28, 1843.

[784] Charles Kelly, born June 25, 1825; lives in Chicago.

[786] Francis, born May 17, 1827; died August 6, 1853, in New Jersey.

[788] Warren H., born December 8, 1830; resides in South Dartmouth, and married Orphia Bennett.

[130-384] GORHAM, son of *William*, was a ship carpenter, residing at South Dartmouth, New Bedford and Providence. He married Phebe V. Soule, of Westport. Had no children.

For a second wife he married Eunice Sears, by whom he had [790] Prince S., [792] Preserved D., [794] Phebe, who married Alfred Washburne, [796] Eunice, who married Edward Curtis, [798] George L.

[142-400] BENJAMIN, son of *Benjamin*, married Eunice Foster, January 8, 1789. Their children were:

[800] Desire, [802] Benjamin, [804] Jonathan; died April 19, 1853, aged sixty.

Sixth Generation. [198-118] HENRY, son of *Peter*, married Elizabeth Grey, of Yarmouth, November 25, 1802; she died in

Boston, December 17, 1846, aged sixty. He organized at Yarmouth, the second temperance society in this country. He was a prominent man in Yarmouth, and was a representative to the General Court at Boston. He died July 29, 1833. His children were :

[812] Eliza Jane, born July 25, 1803, married Nathaniel S. Simpkins, of Yarmouth, May 1824; she died August 30, 1836.

[814] Henry Gray, born April 15, 1805; died January 10, 1833.

[816] Winslow Lewis, born June 27, 1807; died April 14, 1834.

[818] Mary Burr, born November 7, 1809; died November 9, 1827.

[820] Sally, born December 22, 1811; died March 19, 1826.

[822] Maria Edith, born April 8, 1814; died August 31, 1837.

[824] George, born December 7, 1816; died December 31, 1835.

[826] Thomas, born June 19, 1819; still living.

[828] Charles, born December 2, 1821; died August 21, 1824.

[830] Caroline, born October 6, 1824, married Rev. John Philander Perry, April 28, 1853; died April, 1868.

[832] Cornelia, born October 6, 1824; died July 20, 1826.

[831] Henry Charles, born October 6, 1829; still living.

[198-422] LEWIS, son of *Peter*, married Sally Hallet, of Yarmouth, August 27, 1805. He was a prominent business man in the village of Hyannis, where he died. Their children were :

[836] Sally Hallet, born June 8, 1806, married Captain Sylvester B. Baxter; she died October 24, 1839.

[838] Olive, born April 2, 1808, married Freeman C. Tobey, of Hyannis, where she still lives.

[840] George Lewis, born November 6, 1809; died May 10, 1833.

[842] Octavia, born July 18, 1811; died ——.

[844] Rebecca Winslow, born July 27, 1813, married Captain Timothy B. Crowell. For a second husband she married Captain William Bearce.

[846] Peter, born January 9, 1816; died December 3, 1831.

[848] Betsey Howes, born May 19, 1818; died Sept. 28, 1820.

[850] Lewis, born September 20, 1824; died February 24, 1825.

[212,421] SAMUEL P. S., son of *Judge George*, was a lawyer, and practiced law at Saco, Maine, but afterwards removed to Mobile, Alabama. He married Jane C. D. Savage, and died at Mobile, November 5, 1852. Their children were:

[852] Joseph Savage, born July 10, 1819; died at Mobile October 31, 1842.

[854] Anthony, born May 15, 1821; died at Mobile Oct. 31, 1842.

[856] Lucy S., born June 3, 1823; married Henry Van Antwerp, of Mobile, June 3, 1841; died ——.

[858] Julia Anna, born October 10, 1825.

[840] Alexander Hamilton, born June 2, 1832; died ——.

[862] Caroline Hubbard, born ——.

[212,428] GEORGE, son of *Judge George*, married his cousin, Lucy Bigelow. He died at Westford, 1857. Their children were:

[861] Anna Bigelow, born January 19, 1819.

[836] Sarah Bigelow, born January 20, 1820.

[864] Anne Savage, born May 22, 1823.

[870] George, born February 23, 1825.

[872] Amelia Hepsibah, born November 30, 1826.

[874] Jane Frances, born September 26, 1828.

[212,132] HENRY SAVAGE, son of *Judge George*, married Elizabeth Haven Wardrobe, of Portsmouth, New Hampshire, Sept. 26, 1822. He, like his father, was very much interested in the genealogy of his family, and did much to collect more material. Their children were:

[876] Eleanor Wardrobe, born July 29, 1823.

[878] Joseph Haven, born February 10, 1825; an apothecary in Portsmouth, New Hampshire.

[""] Henry Savage, born December 11, 1826.

[882] John Wardrobe, born November 4, 1829; resides in Shirley, Massachusetts.

[884] Walter Irvine,¹ born January 2, 1832.

[886] Nathan Parker, born December 17, 1833.

[888] Ann Wentworth, born August 9, 1835.

[890] Emily Irvine, born October 16, 1837.

[892] Walter Irvine,[2] born July 27, 1839; resides in Boston.

[212-434] LEWIS, son of *Judge George*, married Mary Goodrich. He died at Babylon, Long Island, 1830. Their children were: [894] Mary Emma, [896] Catherine De Wolf, [898] Leonard, [900] Lewis.

[212-438] JOSIAH, son of *Judge George*, married Jane Scammon, died at Biddeford, Maine, in 1836. Their children were: [902] Rebecca Winslow.[1]   [904] Josiah Winslow.

[906] Rebecca Winslow,[2] born October 24, 1825.

[908] Angela, born June 22, 1828.

[910] Lucy Savage, born June 4, 1831.

[912] Martha Buckminster, born February 8, 1833.

[214-450] THOMAS, son of *Colonel Thomas*, married Caroline, daughter of Samuel Billings, of Boston. Their children were: [914] Thomas, born January 8, 1824, married Marietta Crooker, to whom was born Hester Billings in 1857; [916] Samuel B., died young.

[918] Mary Anner, born ——, died October 15, 1838.

[920] Hester Billings, born October 15, 1831, married William Beecher, October 19, 1853; died October 25, 1853.

[922] Caroline Billings, born November 5, 1833.

[924] William Gill, born July 28, 1846.

[214-452] GEORGE C., son of *Colonel Thomas*, married Maria W. Howard. He died October 21, 1856. Their children were: [926] George Thomas, born July 8, 1827.

[928] Charles Augustus, born September 4, 1829.

[930] James Edward, born September 21, 1832.

[932] Fredrick H.   [934] Alfred C., born December 1, 1836.

[936] Frank H.   [938] Henry Howard.

[260]_[178] SAMUEL, son of *John*, married and resided at Barnstable, where he died in 1870. Their children were:

[910] Samuel Wells, born January 31, ———.

[912] William Martin, born February 7, 1836.

[911] Henry B., born May 13. 1841.

[916] Francis, born April 14, 1845.

[260]_[480] JOHN, son of *John*, married Eliza Hewitt, of Ipswich, August 3, 1815. He died January 17, 1827. Their children were :

[948] Eliza Ann, born June 3, 1816, married [612] Edward Thacher.

[950] Hannah Bourne, born January, 1819, married [612] Edward Thacher.

[952] James, born November 28, 1821.

[276]_[500] TIMOTHY, eldest son of *Deacon Roland*, was born at Wareham, but removed in early life to Lee, Berkshire county. He married Dolly (Dorotha) Phelps, of Marlboro', December 31, 1799, and died at Lee October 30, 1833, aged sixty years. Their children were:

[954] Crocker, born October 9, 1800; died October 16, 1863.

[956] Charles Stone, born May 5, 1802; died December 14. 1869.

[958] Betsey F., born January 23, 1804 ; died March 28, 1820.

[960] Buckley, born February 22, 1806; died September 16, 1863.

[962] Adah E.,* born February 25, 1808, married Seth D. Graves : still living at Hartford.

[964] Eliel Tobey, born February 12, 1812; still living at Lee.

[966] Martha,† born February 5, 1815, married John Sears, of Lenox, Massachusetts. Lives in Illinois.

[276]_[506] ROLAND, son of *Deacon Roland*, married for his first wife, Betsey Freeman, of Lee, March 24, 1803. She died February, 1804. He afterwards married Lucretia Hinckley, November 20, 1805. He died May 5, 1809. Their children were:

---

* See Appendix.   † Ibid.

[968] Lucy, born November 16, 1806; died ——.
[970] Roland, born 1808; died December 30, 1828.

[275-510] STEPHEN, son of *Deacon Roland*, was born at Wareham, Barnstable county, Massachusetts, March 6, 1781, where he lived until he was seventeen years of age, when his father decided to remove to Lee, Berkshire county, whither some of his friends and acquaintances had already gone. Having determined to remove, the question of *how* and *when* became the all important one, for in those days railroads were unknown, and a journey of one hundred and fifty miles was as much of an undertaking as a journey from Boston to San Francisco would be now. It was finally decided to move in February, while sleighing was good. Accordingly a large ox sled was provided, upon which the household goods—the *Lares* and *Penates*—were loaded, and which was drawn by a yoke of oxen with a horse at the lead. They started about the twentieth day of February, and were seventeen days on the journey, striking the Boston and Albany turnpike—the great thoroughfare of those days—near Worcester. So long were they on this road, that the same stages and drivers passed and repassed them several times on their trip between Boston and Albany. They arrived at their destination on Saturday. News of their coming had preceded them, and a company of their old friends came out to escort them in, meeting them near what is known as "Green-Water Pond," in the town of Becket. His father purchased a farm of about three hundred acres, a little north of the village of Lee, on which Stephen remained for three years, and then determined to ship as a whaler, which was then a very profitable business. Accordingly in the spring of 1801, he went to Hudson, New York, for that purpose, but finding no immediate chance to ship, he procured work, intending to remain there until a good opportunity offered itself. None however offering, he returned home in the autumn, where he remained till the following spring, when he, in company with others, engaged to labor on the turnpike then

being built between Albany and Schenectady, New York. He continued in this business five seasons of seven months each, a part of the time as overseer. Returning to Lee he engaged in manufactures, and was the pioneer in several important enterprises, building a powder mill, which he carried on until the embargo of 1809 caused its suspension in 1811. He also built a wire factory, and continued the manufacture of wire until after the war of 1812, when English wire coming in, he could not compete with it. He also built and carried on a chair factory for several years. He built the first paper mill on the Housatonic river in Lee, and remained in this business until his retirement from active life in 1852. In connection with this he established the manufacture and sale of Navarrino bonnets, which were very fashionable and popular at one time, and which proved for a season a very profitable business. His mind, always active and of an inventive turn, was continually seeking to improve upon the methods he then possessed, and he introduced many useful improvements in the manufacture of paper, some of which are still used. Not content with the manner of manufacturing paper, a sheet at a time, and by hand, he conceived the idea of making it in a continuous sheet and by machinery, and obtained a reluctant consent and an appropriation of fifteen hundred dollars of his partners to experiment in that direction. The result was that in less than six weeks, and before the appropriation was used up, he presented a sheet of paper of the ordinary width, and several feet in length to his partners, who were speechless with astonishment. This was the origin of the cylinder machine for making paper, which is still used in many mills, and of which he was the inventor.

He possessed the confidence and esteem of the entire community, and was honored with many important trusts. He was appointed Justice of the Peace for seven successive terms—twenty-eight years in all, and was known by the title of "Squire" Thatcher so long, that his given name was almost forgotten, and in fact unknown by many. He was elected to the legislature of Massachusetts for two years, 1829 and '31, and while there was the originator of measure that were of much value to manufacturers, especially owners of mill sites. In the year 1852, being somewhat advanced in years, and desirous of retiring from active business, he sold out his interests in Lee and removed to Saratoga Springs, where he now resides (May 1, 1872), at the advanced age of ninety-one.

He married Hannah Basset, of Lee, July 2, 1806. She died at Lee, September 14, 1848. Their children were:

[971] Maria Louisa, born December 25, 1809, married Jared Ingersoll, November 15, 1832; resides at Saratoga Springs.

[976] George, born September 12, 1811, married Eliza M. Brown, October 3, 1833; died at Lee, March 17, 1852, leaving no children.

[978] Caroline, born April 28, 1821, married Dr. Horatio S. Cobb, November 11, 1847; he died at Sacramento, California, of cholera, while in practice in that city, October 25, 1850.

[288-516] DAVID, son of *Lot*, married Deborah Deblois, of Newport, Rhode Island. Their children were:

[980] Stephen D., who married Miss Dennison.

[982] Sarah, who married Charles Locke, resides in Cambridge.

[984] George, died unmarried.

[986] Edward H., living in New York city.

[988] Harriet, married William H. Bartlett, of Newburyport; afterward to John J. Adams, now of New York.

[990] Anne, married first Henry Gibson, afterwards George McDonald, of New York.

[288-524] CHARLES F., son of *Lot*, married Sylvia Crocker, of Hanover. Was a farmer living in Middleboro'; died in 1871. Their children were:

[992] Charles T., married Sophia Barrows, of Middleboro'; died December 13, 1850. He had Fredrick C., who died young.

[994] Caroline A., married Stephen D. Jordan, of New Bedford.

[996] Eliza S., married Horatio Wood.

[998] Sarah B., married James H. Sampson; died April, 1872.

[1000] Annie M., died unmarried.

[1002] Priscilla, died unmarried.

[1004] Adelaide M., died unmarried, December, 1851.

[1006] William H., a mariner, living, unmarried.

[1006] Mary C., married James B. Sears, of Rochester.

[288-526] PETER, son of *Lot*, was born at Wareham; resided for a time at Middleboro', and then removed to Boston and engaged for a time in mercantile pursuits. He afterward, in company with his brother, under the title of David & Peter Thatcher, carried on a heavy dry goods business, and in 1849 the firm became Thatcher & Fearing. There was at the same time another firm bearing the title of Fearing & Thacher ([620] Isaac). In later years he was engaged in the insurance business. He married, December 9, 1815, Elizabeth Fearing, of Wareham. She died in Boston, March 31, 1864, aged sixty-nine.

He still resides in Boston, with his son, Franklin N., at the age of eighty-two. Their children were:

[1010] John Fearing, born September 7, 1818; married Catharine Burgiss, of Fair Haven, August 28, 1843, and had children.

[1012] Elizabeth Fearing, born January 29, 1822; married Wilson J. Welsh, now of Newton Centre, Massachusetts.

[1014] Peter Fearing, born May 13, 1824; practiced medicine in Boston; died August 6, 1847, unmarried.

[1016] Emmeline H., born March 31, 1826; died March 5, 1838.

[1018] George A., born ———; died November 20, 1842.

[1020] Albert E., born May 22, 1829; reporter for New York Evening Express.

[1022] Franklin N., born October 1, 1835; lives in Boston.

[288-522] ALLEN, son of *Lot*, is a farmer, and resides in Middleboro'. He married Elizabeth R. Peirce, December 7, 1816. Their children were:

[1024] Levi, P.,[1] born May 2, 1818; died August 12, 1823.

[1026] Levi P.,[2] married Sarah Darrow, of Boston, and had Henry Lincoln.

[1028] Elizabeth Allen, married Robert K. Remington, of Fall River.

[288-534] ISRAEL FEARING, son of *Lot*, resides in Middleboro'. He married Susan Wood. Their children were:

[1030] Nelson W., who is married and has one daughter.

[1032] Lewis, married Miss —— Thompson. No children.

[1034] Frances, married. Has no children.

[1036] Henry, married Miss —— Allen.

[1038] Susan, married Captain Reuben Briggs.

[300-566] SAMUEL, son of *Solomon*, married Nancy Hallet, of Yarmouth, ——, 1808. She died June 19, 1862, aged seventy-five. He died October, 1871, and was a deacon of the church at Yarmouth. Their children were:

[1040] Samuel, born November 8, 1809; resides at Yarmouth.

[1042] Solomon, born February 13, 1813; resides in Harwich.

[1044] Watson, born September 11, 1816; resides in Yarmouth.

[1046] Nancy, born April 7, 1822; married Gorham Bray.

[1048] Sarah, born May 2, 1825; married David G. Eldridge.

[300-574] BENJAMIN, son of *Solomon*, was a blacksmith; resided at South Dennis; was a prominent man, and held the principal town offices at different times. He married, first, Sukey S. Hopkins, of Brewster, April 2, 1818. She died Sept. 8, 1819, aged 25. He married, second, Amanda Baker, of West Dennis. She died Feb. 20, 1835. Their children wore :

[1050] Benjamin, born March 3, 1821; resides in West Dennis.

[1052] Prentiss, born Oct. 1, 1822.

Sukey Snow, born July 21, 1824; married Daniel Baker, now of Chester, Pa.

[1051] Joseph F., born June 10, 1826 ; resides in West Dennis.

[1056] Ezra, born May 12, 1829 ; resides in West Dennis.

[1058] Mary Ann, born October 10, 1831 ; married Henry K. White. She died Aug. 17, 1856.

[1060] John Gorham, born June 4, 1833 ; resides in Yarmouth. He married, for a third wife, Nancy Nickerson, of West Dennis, May 3, 1835, and had one child [1062] Olive, born Jan. 25, 1836, married Ansel C. Collins, Jan. 6, 1858 ; died at Philadelphia, June 23, 1858.

[304-576] PELEG, son of *Ebenezer*, was a master mariner, and married Betty Hallet, of Yarmouth. Their children were :

[1064] Alfred, born October 22, 1813, married Miss Livingston ; has children, and resides near Galena, Ill.

[1066] Eleanor, born May 28, 1815 ; died about 1839.

[301-578] LOTHROP TAYLOR, son of *Ebenezer*, was a master mariner, married Thankful Nickerson, of Yarmouth, in 1812. Their children were :

[1068] Emeline, born October 9, 1813, married Seth Whilden of South Dennis.

[1070] Lothrop.   [1072] Anthony, born May 23, 1820, died April 7, 1866.

[1074] George E., master mariner, resides in Dennis.

[310-596] JOSEPH, son of *Joseph* and *Phebe Gage*, of Yarmouth. in 1811. He was a master mariner, and died at sea in 1823. Their children were :

[1076] Joseph (¹) Freeman, born January 12, 1817 ; died Sept. 5, 1821.

[1078] Patia, born March 27, 1823, died 1823.

[1080] Joseph (²), born March 27, 1823, died 1823.

[318-612] BARNABAS, son of *Barnabas* ; married Mary Gray, of Yarmouth, Aug. 13, 1822. Their children were :

[1082] Mary G., born July 15, 1823, in Brewster, married Dr. Clark.

[1084] Rebecca, born Feb. 11, 1825, at Brewster, married — Morrison, of Boston.

[1086] Joseph, born Oct. 10, 1827, at Barnstable; died at Lake Superior.

[1088] Charles Gray, born Oct. 2, 1830, married Eliza J. Snow, of Yarmouth, where he resides.

[1090] Charlotte, born Sept. 27, 1836, died Oct. 4, 1836.

[318.614] EDWARD, son of *Barnabas*, was a manufacturer of railroad spikes in Boston, and later had saltworks in Charlestown. He died at Yarmouth in 1871. He married, first, Lydia T. Gray, of Yarmouth, Aug. 13, 1822. She died July 4, 1835, aged 33. Their children were:

[1092] Warren, born Nov. 26, 1823, died Sept. 15, 1852.

[1094] Joshua (1) born March 12, 1825, died Sept. 12, 1826.

[1096] Martha, born Feb. 25, 1827; living at Yarmouth.

[1098] Joshua G (2), born April 18, 1829; died May 19.

[1100] Joshua G (3) born May 28, 1830; died Feb. 27, 1866. He married Melinda Crowell, and had Warren, born July 7, 1858.

[1102] Edward, born Aug. 11, 1832; died Nov. 10, 1858.

[1104] Lydia Gray, born May 30, 1835; married Nehemiah N. Hinckley, of Dennis, Dec. 8, 1858.

For second wife he married [948] Eliza A. Thacher. She died in Boston, March, 1852. They had one child [1106] Gertrude, born Aug. 5, 1839, married Capt. Henry Arey, of Yarmouth, Aug. 30, 1860.

For a third wife he married [950] Hannah B. Thacher.

[314.620] ISAAC, son of *Barnabas*, is a merchant, and is noted for his liberality and benevolence. He married a lady in Boston, by whom he had [1108] Sarah, [1110] George.

[332.621] LOTHROP RUSSELL, son of *David*, was a successful

merchant in Boston until the embargo of 1812, which obliged him to suspend business there. He afterwards moved to Philadelphia. Died at sea and was buried on Staten Island. He married Ann Bowditch. Their children were :

1112 William Russell, 1114 Sarah, 1116 Ann.

340-680 PADDOCK, son of *Josiah*, married Lucy Hallet, of Yarmouth, Feb. 28, 1822. She died March, 1872. He died Dec. 25, 1867, at Yarmouth. Their children were :

1118 Russell (1) born April 13, 1823, died Aug. 4, 1823.

1120 Harriet H., born Sept. 28, 1825, died Oct. 14, 1826.

1122 Russell (2) born April 26, 1827. Married Harriet Cobb, of Barnstable. He was drowned at sea April 17, 1855.

1124 Phebe, born Feb. 16, 1829, married David S. Russell. Died Aug. 21, 1862.

1126 Oliver, born May 26, 1832, married Hannah G. Crowell, by whom he had Anna H., born Nov. 22, 1857, and Lucy O., born Dec. 6, 1856. He died July 8, 1866.

1128 Azubah Hallet, born May 25, 1835, married Simeon H. Brown, of Boston, Died April 13. 1860.

1130 Lucy Ellen, born Nov. 3, 1837, died June 1, 1839.

340-682 JOSIAH, son of *Josiah*, married Daty Barker. Their children were 1132 Lydia Hedge, resides in Brooklyn, L. I., 1134 Josiah, 1136 Daty Ann, 1137 William, 1140 George.

826-721 ISAIAH C, son of *Mathews*, graduate at Union College, in 1841, and also New Haven Theological Seminary. He was ordained as Congregational minister at Matapoisett, Mass., Dec. 25, 1844. He now resides at Wareham (Parker Mills) and is pastor of the same society, which the 114 Rev. Roland, his mother's grandfather, was in 1740. He married, first, Elizabeth K. Hyde; she died at Central Falls, N. Y., Nov. 24, 1848. They had—

1142 Mary Ludlow, born Jan. 28, 1846; died Dec. 10, 1861.

For a second wife he married Mary C. Hyde, Oct. 24, 1849. She died Aug. 27, 1865. They had—

[1144] Charles Mathews, born Aug. 10, 1851; residence in Gloucester.

[1146] Elizabeth Hyde, born April 9, 1853; died April 7, 1854.

[1148] Anna Russell, born May 15, 1855.

[1150] Harriet Serena, born Jan. 30, 1858. He adopted his brother, H. M. Thacher's son [1152] George Hungerford, born Feb. 15, 1865. For a third wife he married Lydia W. Proctor, Nov. 21, 1866.

[372-740] DAVIS, son of *Laban*, was a ship carpenter at Dartmouth and Fair Haven; married Mary Nye, of Fair Haven, June 1, 1819. Their children were:

[1154] Sally Davis, born 1822; married Chas. T. Tobey.

[1156] Watson, born April 30, 1824; died at sea Sept. 24, 1844.

[1158] Susan Nye, born March 3 1826.

[1160] Sylvia Nye, born ——, 1827 : married Joseph Manchester.

[1162] Isaac Warren, born June 13, 1835.

[1164] Eliza Ann, born 1830; married Franklin Nye.

[372-744] LABAN, Jr., son of *Laban*, married Abiah Carey. He died Jan., 1839, at New Bedford. Their children were:

[1166] Horatio ——. [1168] Edward; died at New Bedford.

[372-748] STEPHEN, son of *Laban*, was a ship master; married Harriet Prince. Their children were:

[1170] Stephen D., who has married twice, and resides at Lawrence, Kansas.

[1172] William, also married.

[1174] Mary Ann, married and has one child.

[372-750] ISAAC, son of *Laban*, was a master mariner, following the sea about forty years, but he now resides at Fairhaven, Mass. He married Eliza A. Howland, Nov. 29, 1827, and had one

son.   [1176] Albert D., who married Mary A. Chase, and had—
Addie. born Feb. 1858; Mabel born June, 1864; Gertrude, born
Sept., 1866.

[372-752] WARREN, son of *Laban*, is a master mariner, and
resides at Fair Haven, Mass.; he married Susan M. Nye, July
7, 1824.   Their children were—

[1178] Otis Freeman, born Aug. 31, 1833; resides at No. Dartmouth.

[1180] Thomas Nye, born Aug. 12, 1840; resides at Chicago.

[380-770] ANTHONY, son of *William*, carried on the fishing
business, in Chatham, where he still resides; he married
Jerusha Ryder of Chatham, and had one son—

[1182] Albert, born 1841, who married Lottie Taylor, of Chatham, and had— [1184] Albert F., born Aug. 26, 1863; [1186] Anthony E. born Sept. 1, 1864; [1188] Walter C., born March 30, 1866.

[100-801] JONATHAN, son of *Benjamin*, was a master mariner,
and resided at Brewster; he married, first, Rhoda S. Lincoln.
of Brewster; she died May 8, 1835, he died April 19, 1853.
aged 60; their children were—

[1190] Benjamin[1] born Aug. 4, 1822, died 1824.

[1192] Benjamin[2] born April 6, 1827, lost at sea, 1864.

For a second wife he married Desire Lincoln.

Seventh Generation.   [418-826] THOMAS, son of *Henry*, was
born at Yarmouth Port, removed to Boston in early life and
engaged in mercantile pursuits, he now lives in New York, and
is a commission merchant.   He married for his first wife, Mary
G. Hallet, of Yarmouth, June 21, 1840.   She died Sept. 18,
1850, aged 28.   Their children were:

[1280] Elizabeth, born at Yarmouth, Sept. 2, 1841; living.

[1212] Charles Hallet, born at Yarmouth, Oct. 27, 1843.

[1204] * George Winslow, born at Boston, Sept. 27, 1848.

[1206] Mary Gorham, born at Boston, Sept. 18, 1850, died Oct. 14th 1850.

For a second wife he married Catherine Worcester, of Boston, Dec. 24, 1851; their children were :

[1208] Alice, born at Boston, June 8, 1853.

[1210] Grace Sanderson, born April 1, 1855.

[1212] Arthur, born at Newtonville, May 8, 1857.

[1214] Anna Worcester, born at Brooklyn, L. I., Sept. 9, 1859.

[1216] Amy Clark, born at Brooklyn, Nov. 11, 1862.

[1218] Thomas Worcester, born at New York, June 15, 1868.

[418-834] HENRY C. son of *Henry*, was born at Yarmouth Port, where he still resides, but carries on business in Boston as a dealer in cotton. He married Martha Bray, of Yarmouth, Dec. 3, 1855; their children were :

[1220] Thomas Chandler, born July 20, 1858.

[1222] Carolne, born July 19, 1860.

[1224] Henry Winslow, born Dec. 29, 1862.

[1226] Walter Gray, born Dec. 8, 1864, died 1870.

[1228] Louis Bartlet, born May 12, 1867.

[1230] Mary, ——.

[1232] Mattie, ——.

[122-840] GEORGE L. son of *Lewis*, was a master mariner, married Martha Baxter, in 1831; he died May 10, 1833.— They had one son :

[1234] Geo. L. born Jan. 14, 1834.

[432-926] GEORGE T. son of *George C. Thacher*, married, in 1872, Anna, daughter of Holmes Hinkley ; resides at Yarmouth Port, and is connected with the Fulton Iron Foundry Co., of Boston.

* We are largely indebted to him for many of the later records comprising this volume.

452-926 CHARLES A., son of *Geo. C.*, married Clara Augusta, daughter of W. R. Austin, of Boston, where he resides.

452-931 ALFRED C., son of *Geo. C.*, married Anna, daughter of Nahum Capen, of Boston, and has :

1240 Geo. Churchill, born June 3, 1862.

1242 Maria Howard, born Mch. 17, 1865.

1244 Elizabeth Moore, born Nov. 21, 1866.

500-954 CROCKER, oldest son of *Timothy*, was born at Lee, Oct. 9, 1800. He was engaged in agricultural pursuits during his life, and was an honored and respected member of the community in which he lived. He died Oct. 16, 1863, at Saratoga Springs, while on a visit to his uncle, Stephen Thatcher. He married Lucy Basset, of Lee and had :

1250 Timothy Dwight, born May 15, 1823 ; still residing at Lee.

500-956 CHARLES STONE, son of *Timothy*, was born at Lee, May 5, 1802, and died at the residence of his daughter Lydia, in Auburn, N. Y., Dec. 14, 1869, aged 67. He was also a farmer, and possessed the confidence and esteem of the community. He was chosen, for one term, to represent his native town at the General Court in Boston, and held other minor offices in the town at different times. He married Atteresta Birchard, of Lee ; he died Oct. 19, 1863. Their children were :

1252 Julia Francis, born Nov. 28, 1825 ; died Jan. 28, 1846.

1254 * Lydia Jane, born Jan. 4, 1827, died May 28, 1871.

1256 Amos Birchard, born June 25, 1828, died Sept. 26, 1866.

1258 Nancy A., born Feb. 1, 1830, died Nov. 28, 1847.

1260 Charles F., born Aug. 21, 1832 ; married Cynthia Bigelow, of Egremont, April. 9, 1862, and died at Lee, Jan. 30, 1869. of consumption, contracted while serving in the army at Port Hudson, (49th Regt., Mass. Vol.). He left two children— Atteresta C., and Nellie E.

* See Appendix.

[1262] Lucy E., born Nov. 26, 1834; married Dr. David W. Allen, of Vineland, N. J., July 1, 1868; died at Vineland, Aug. 22, 1869.

[1264] George A., born Aug. 13, 1836; married in 1869, to Miss Fanny P. McKean, resides at Albany, N. Y.

[1266] Julian D., born Nov. 19, 1838; died Oct., 23, 1842.

[1268] Reumah Grace, born Dec. 8, 1841; resides at Auburn, N. Y.

[1270] Julian Adler, born Nov. 10, 1845; resides at Albany, N. Y.

[500_960] BUCKLEY, son of *Timothy*, was born at Lee, Feb. 22, 1806; married Emerancy Culver, April 6, 1830, and removed to Litchfield, Ohio, where his descendants now reside. He was killed Sept. 16, 1853, by a R. R. accident, near Oneida, N. Y., while returning home from a visit to his friends in Massachusetts. Their children were:

[1272] Roland Crocker, born July 17, 1832.

[1274] James Gilbert, born July 13, 1834.

[1276] Cynthia Melvina, born Feb. 23, 1837; married Rolin W. Cole, April 6, 1857; died April 19, 1858.

[1278] George Edward, born April 3, 1839; died July 9, 1840.

[1280] Martha Orilla, born July 27, 1841; married Simon Seeley, Nov. 11, 1866; they have one daughter, Izella Eliza, born Oct. 18, 1867.

[1282] Sarah Emeline, born Jan. 3, 1844; married Frank Fairchilds, Sept. 14, 1871.

[1284] Abigail Antonette, born April 11, 1846.

[1286] Charles Phelps, born March 7, 1848; married Elida Packard, Sept. 12, 1871.

[1288] Timothy Dwight, born March 2, 1850; married Flora Blanchard, Aug. 4, 1870.

[500_964] ELIEL T., son of *Timothy*, was born Feb. 12, 1812, and resides at Lee, where he is engaged in mechanical pursuits.

He married, first, Emeline Gale, of Hadley; she died Aug. 10, 1840. They had— ·

[1290] Lucy, born July 4, 1835; died Nov. 10, 1840.

He afterward married Diantha Stebbins, of Belchertown,; she died Aug. 29, 1864. Their children were:

[1292] Harriet B., born April 17, 1838; resides at Lee.

[1294] Emeline G., born May 13, 1840; married Feb. 8, 1872, to Janus M. Fuary, of West Stockbridge.

[526_1022] FRANKLIN N. son of *Peter*, grandson of [28] Lot, resides in Boston. He married Eunice H. Cheney, June 6, 1865. Their children were:

[1296] Elizabeth F., born March 28. 1866.

[1298] Sarah Ann, born Dec. 22, 1869; died Nov. 2, 1870.

[561_1010] SAMUEL, son of *Samuel*, married Polly Hamblin, in 1833, and resides at Yarmouth. Their children were:

[1300] Edwin, born Aug. 30, 1835; married Elizabeth T. Mathews, of Yarmouth, March 8, 1860.

[1302] Cyrus, born Sept 3, 1837.

[1304] Mary Hamblin, born July 12, 1839.

[1306] Samuel H., born Aug., 17, 1841; married Betsey A. K. Hamblin of Yarmouth, Oct. 10, 1865, and has Geo. Henry, born June 14, 1867.

[1308] Lawrence, born April 1, 1844; lost from ship "Renown," March, 19, 1862, on passage from San Francisco to Callao.

[1310] Isaac H., ([1]) born Jan. 27, 1847; died May 24, 1847.

[1312] Benjamin H., born March 26, 1849.

[1314] Emma Watson, born April 20, 1851.

[1316] Isaac H. ([2]) born July 13, 1853.

[566_1012] SOLOMON, son of *Samuel*, married Mercy Welden. Their children were:

[1318] Mary Gray, born July 22, 1839; married Gustavus C. Robbins, of Harwich, Nov, 1865.

[1320] George, born March 15, 1844, died May 11, 1848.

[566-1044] WATSON, son of *Samuel*; married Emeline Hamblin, of Yarmouth, in 1841. They have:

[1322] Franklin, born April 30, 1842; married, first, Isabella Mathews; she died Aug. 2, 1867, leaving a son; for a second wife he married Eleanor P. Knowles of Yarmouth.

[574-1050] BENJAMIN, son of *Benjamin*, married Nancy B. Nickerson, Dec. 17, 1843. Their children were:

[1324] Thomas Snow, born Sept. 12, 1844.

[1326] Eleazer Nickerson, born Sept. 20, 1846.

[1328] Benjamin F., born May 19, 1852.

[1330] Henry, born June 15, 1856.

[1332] Willis ——.

[1334] Joseph Lucas, ——,

[571-1052] PRENTISS, son of *Benjamin*, married Dinah Hall Nickerson, Oct. 21, 1844. Their children were:

[1336] Ellen, born May 2, 1846.

[1338] George P. born April 1, 1848.

[1340] Josiah Hedge, born Sept. 11, 1850.

[1342] Oliver, born March 23, 1854.

[574-1060] JOHN G., son of *Benjamin*, married Almira Gorham, of Yarmouth, where he now resides; Their children were:

[1344] John, born Jan. 29, 1860.

[1346] Sarah White, born Oct. 6, 1863.

[1348] William Hallet, born Oct. 5, 1866.

[578-1072] ANTHONY, son of *Lothrop S.*, married Martha Blodgett, of Stafford, Con., April 12, 1828. He was a master mariner, and died April 7, 1866. Their children were:

[1350] Blanche, born Sept. 26, 1847; married Marcius M. Fisk, now of Allegany, Pa.

[1352] Charlotte Gould, born Sept. 12, 1850.
[1354] Francis Hyde, born Jan. 22, 1854.
[1356] Jenny Maud, born March 21, 1857.

[752-1178] OTIS FREEMAN, son of *Warren O.*, married Mercy J. Dennis, and has one son :

[1358] William Warren, born July 17, 1865.

Eighth Generation. [840-1234] GEORGE L. son of *George L.* married Elizabeth Crowell, of Barnstable, Jan. 14, 1852. Their children are :

[1360] Peter, born 1852.
[1362] George L., born Oct. 1, 1860.

For a second wife he married Miss — Bearse.

[954-1250] TIMOTHY DWIGHT, son of *Crocker*, was born at Lee, May 15, 1823; married for his first wife, Esther Barlow, of Lee. For a second wife he married Harriet F. Clark of Tyringham, Dec. 16, 1846. Their children are :

[1364] Gershom Wesley, born Nov. 6, 1849 ; married April 24, 1872, to Lucy, daughter of Harrison Garfield, Esq., of Lee.
[1366] Mary Ann, born May 4, 1851, died March 17, 1866.
[1368] Francis Dwight, born Dec. 3, 1852.
[1370] Sarah Orphania, born March 5, 1855, died May 1, 1866.
[1372] Lucy Celire, born April 7, 1857.
[1374] Willis Burdette, born Sept. 22, 1859, died July 13, 1866.
[1376] Roland Crocker, born Dec. 9, 1863, died June 19, 1869.
[1378] Hiram Irving, born Feb 10, 1866, died Aug. 30, 1866.
[1380] Herbert Ellsworth, born Oct. 28, 1867.

[969-1272] ROLAND CROCKER, oldest son of *Buckley*, was born July 17. 1832; married Esther L. Nickerson, March 27, 1855, and resides at Litchfield Ohio. Their children are :

[1382] Lilla Gertrude, born April 15, 1856.

[1384] William Churchill, born May 9, 1860.

[1386] Marion Darling, born July 2, 1864.

[1388] Alva Carey, born Aug. 17 1868.

[962-1274] JAMES GILBERT, son of *Buckley*, was born July 13, 1834; married Eliza W. Nickerson, Feb. 4, 1857; resides at Litchfield, Ohio. Their children are:

[1390] Edith Melvina, born Sept. 18, 1859.

[1392] Vernon Ellsworth, born Oct. 1, 1862.

[1394] Orlo Churchill, born March 30, 1865.

[1040-1302] CYRUS, son of *Samuel*, married Lucy G. Taylor of Yarmouth, Nov. 25, 1858. Their children are:

[1396] Caroline, born March 11, 1860.

[1398] William, born Sept. 3, 1866.

The following obituary of [237] Hon. Stephen Thacher (see page 17) was received too late for insertion in its proper place, and we insert it here:

STEPHEN THACHER,

BORN,

At Lebanon, Conn., *January* 9, 1774. Graduated at Yale College, September 9, 1795. Fifth in descent from Peter Thacher, Rector of St. Edmunds, at Salisbury, England, through his son, Thomas, first Minister of the Old South Church, in Boston, Mass.

DIED,

At Rockland, Maine, *February* 9, 1859.

A true Philanthropist, he detested slavery. Ardently loving liberty, he was, through life, enthusiastically devoted to the emancipation of the colored race. Gifted, conscientious, industrious, energetic, resolute; "He scorned delights and lived laborious days."

Scholar, Patriot, Christian! thy long career, full of useful service to thy day and generation, illustrates the virtues of the Puritan Ancestry thou didst revere.

> "*Cui Pudor et Justitiae soror*
> *Incorrupta Fides, nudaque Veritas,*
> *Quando ullum inveniet parem?*
> *Multis ille bonis flebilis occidit.*"
>
> *Hor. Ode.* 24.

We have, also, to record the death of [97] Caroline Thatcher Cobb, (see page 71), of Saratoga Springs, who died at Poughkeepsie, May 21, 1872, after a short illness. She was very much interested in the genealogy of the Thacher family, and to her, and her father, the family are largely indebted for the production of this little volume.

This completes the records of the family as far as we have been able to obtain them. It is, we believe, very nearly a full record of Antony Thacher's descendants, bearing the name of Thacher. They are becoming more widely scattered each year, though very many of them still reside at Yarmouth, and other towns on the Cape, and we learn from Geo. T. Thacher, Esq., that he retains some fifty acres of land that was granted to Antony, in 1638, it never having been out of the family, and that the house built by John Thacher, in 1680, still stands: also that a button pear tree, said to have been planted by Antony, still lives and bears fruit. At the request of several members of the family, we would suggest to those who may be living, in 1885, (the 250th anniversary of the coming of Antony and Thomas) that a family gathering of their descendants be held at Yarmouth, at that time.

APPENDIX.

The following are records of families directly descended from the Thachers, more particularly from Rev. Roland.

HOWLAND.

[52] *Martha F.* eldest daughter of [114] Rev. Roland Thatcher, m. Nathaniel Howland, (see p. 43). They had:

[1] *Sylvia*, b. Nov. 2, 1763; m. Wally Goodspeed, of Sandwich, d. Nov. 4, 1825. They had six children, viz:
Obed, Harrison, Celia, Thomas, Joseph, Lucy.

[2] *Roland*, ([1]) b. Jan. 12, 1766; d. Apl. 27, 1769.

[3] *Lucy*, b. June 23, 1769; m. John Fairfield; d. at Pittsfield. Mass.

[4] *Roland*, ([2]) b. Aug. 19, 1770; d. at sea of yellow fever.

[5] *Martha*, b. Aug. 28, 1772; m. John Howland, of Barnsta-ble, where she died. Had seven children, viz:
Thomas, Roland, Weston, Nathaniel, Lucy, (m. Thomas Goodspeed), David and Martha.

[6] *Abigail*, b. May 12, 1775; d. June 30, 1779.

[7] *Rebecca*, b. June 19, 1777; died 1859, unmarried.

[8] *Abigail T.* b. Sept. 7, 1779; married Gershom Bassett, of Lee, removed to Ohio; d. June 24, 1865; had five children viz:
Lucy H. (b. Feb. 20, 1803, m. [954] Crocker Thatcher, of Lee). Mary Anna, b. Aug. 14, 1806, m. Freeman Nye, Sophronia, b. March 14, 1811; m. Lyman Cunningham, Roxanna H., William N. C.

[9] *Elizabeth*, b. June 15, 1782, m. John Fairfield, at Suffolk, Conn., Aug. 1859.

[10] *James*, b. May 22, 1786; m. Ruth, dau. of Prince Fish, of Sandwich, removed to Lee, Mass., 18—, d. 1846. He died 1852. They had:

[1] *Roland G.*, m. Sarah —— ; removed to Quincy, Ill., died at the insane asylum, Jacksonville, Ill., aged 52. They had:
Sophia, William, Edward, Charles.

[2] *Crocker T.*, b. Sept. 30, 1819; m. Lucy S. Barlow, April 9, 1848; she d. Oct. 20, 1870. They had:

Chas. D., b. Aug. 14, 1849, Esther B., b. Jan. 22, 1854, d. Sept. 21, 1865, Clara A. b. Oct. 17, 1856, William C., b. Aug. 21, 1860.

[3] *Nathaniel*, b. 1821, d. Jan. 1869; unmarried.

[4] *Harrison*, b. Nov. 11, 1825; married Lucina Stedman, Nov. 29, 1846; she d. Sep. 16, 1868. They had:

Emma E. b. July 16, 1850, m. Jas. W. Smith, of Pittsfield, Mass., July 17, 1870.

Lottie R., b. Sept. 30, 1852; d. March 14, 1866; he married second, Eliza L. Baker, Jan. 9, 1870.

NYE.

[281] *Desire*, dau. of Rev. Roland Thatcher, (see p. 43), m. David Nye, of Rochester, Mass. They had:

David, b. 1785; m. Lucy Fearing, of Wareham; he d. at Albany, N. Y., May 9, 1863; she died at Rhinebeck, N. Y., Feb. 22, 1868. They had:

[1] *David*, m., resides in California.

[2] *Desire*, m. Alfred Wilde, resides at Rhinebeck. They have: Fannie, Mary, Lucy and Harry.

[3] *Lucy* died young.

[4] *Mary* m. Capt. William Nott.

[5] *Israel* m. and resides in California.

SWIFT.

[14] *Lucy*, oldest dau. of [26] Jethro and [26] Hannah Thatcher, (see p. 53), m. Ebenezer Swift. They had:

[1] *Lydia*, b. Nov. 7, 1800, d. March 28, 1801.

[2] *Thatcher*, b. Dec. 7, 1802; d. at Charleston, S. C. Aug. 12, 1823

[3] *Nancy*, b. Dec. 27, 1804; m. Ephraim Hanchett, of Canaan, Conn., June 5, 1826. Had five children, viz:

Lucy S., Mary H., Nancy L., Nancy S., Thatcher S.

[4] *Lydia*, b. May 7, 1807, m. Jabez Perry. Has nine children, viz:

Lydia, Solomon, Lucy S., Jabez W., Hannah M., Ebenezer S., Martha R., Henry C. and Ellis B.

[5] *Martha T.* born Nov. 20, 1810 ; m. Roland Thatcher Gibbs, resides at Kings Ferry, Cayuga Co., N. Y.

OLMSTEAD.

[476] *Sophia,* youngest dau. of [256] Jethro and [286] Hannah Thatcher (see p. 53), m. Leonard Olmstead, at Lee, Feb. 5, 1816 ; he died at Camden, N. Y., Jan. 3, 1849, aged 58 ; she died at Elmira, N. Y., Feb. 29, 1860, aged 68. They had :

[1] *Lucy A.,* b. in Stockbridge, Apl. 3, 1817 ; m. Aaron Chapin of Lee, Jan. 22, 1835 ; have five children, viz : Lucy V., b. July 23, 1837 ; m. Joel S. Page. Sophia N., b. Jan. 20, 1839 ; m. Samuel N. Benedict ; resides at Hartford, Conn. ; Howard C. b. Feb. 21, 1841, resides in Colorado ; Samuel L., b. Jan. 11, 1844 ; William H. b. May 28, 1847.

BRIGGS.

[304] *Abigail,* dau. of [276] Dea. Roland Thatcher, (see p. 57) m. Joshua Briggs, of Wareham ; he died July 21, 1830. They had :

[1] *Elizabeth,* b. blind, Dec. 10, 1812 ; d. Oct. 2, 1834.

[2] *Harriet,* b. Nov. 13, 1816 ; m. Enoch Comstock, of Lee, May 21, 1840, and resides in Quincy, Ill. They had : Frances, b. Oct. 10, 1841 ; d. June 29, 1842 ; Ellen, b. Apl. 25, 1847 ; Gertrude, b. June 11, 1849 ; Charles Gilbert, b. Feb. 18, 1855.

GRAVES.

[962] *Adah E.,* dau. of [500] Timothy Thatcher, m. Seth D. Graves, of Lee, Dec. 10, 1833, (see p. 68). They had :

[1] *Miles Wells,* b. at Lee, Mass., Nov. 29, 1834 ; m. Ruth Wade, of Hartford, Conn., Oct. 5, 1864 ; he is at present Cashier of the Conn. River Banking Co., of Hartford.

[2] *Julia A.* b. at Lee, Aug. 27, 1836.

[3] *Lemuel Clark,* b. July 9, 1838 ; m. Jane E. Frost, of Waterbury, Conn., Nov. 3, 1864. They have two children : Frank Wells, b. March 24, 1868, and Clifford Lemuel, b. Oct. 21, 1869.

[4] *Martha Marilla,* b. Sept. 27, 1840 ; d. Sept. 15, 1867.

[5] *Emma Eliza*, b. July 7, 1845, m. at Lee, Mass., Dec. 8, 1869, to Geo. F. Washburn, of Lenox, Mass.

SEARS.

[966] *Martha*, youngest dau. of [5m] Timothy Thatcher, (see p. 68) m. John Sears, of Lenox, Mass., Feb. 10, 1837, and removed to Illinois. They had:

[1] *Samuel*, b. Feb. 22, 1838; m. Martha Brooker, and have Wells R., b. Jan. 12, 1868.

[2] *Betsey T.*, b. Feb. 10, 1840; d. Feb. 2, 1841.

[3] *Adah E*, Nov. 2, 1844; m. John Radio, May 10, 1864.— They have John E. b. Jan. 5, 1869, Lena T. b. Feb. 5, 1871.

[4] *Fanny J.* b. Jan. 5, 1846, m. Vincent Shank, Dec. 10, 1867. They have Jennie M., b. Nov. 27, 1868., Ida May, b. March 27, 1870.

[5] *Gilbert J.*, b. Oct. 21, 1848.

[6] *Edwin M.* b. Sept. 27, 1851.

WRIGHT.

[1251] *Lydia J.* dau. of [956] Charles S. Thatcher, (see p. 80) m. Dr. George B. Wright of Lee, July 19, 1852, and settled in Auburn, New York, where she died, May 28, 1871. They had:

[1] *George B., Jr.*, b. Apl. 14, 1853.

[2] *Frank S.*, b. Feb. 23, 1858.

[3] *Charles Fred*, b. Aug. 20, 1860.

[4] *Louie Grace*, b. Feb. 20, 1862.

ERRATA.

Page 26, for 275-265, read 275-369.

Page 27, top line, for 1682 read 1632.

Page 33, third line, for Bethian, read Bethiah.

Page 53, for 108-216, read 108-260.

Page 56, for 410-270, read 110-270.

Page 57, for 116-288, read 114-288.

Page 69, for 275-510, read 276-508.

Page 74, in line commencing 310-596, &c., for *and* read *married*.

Page 76, for 866-724, read 366-724.

Page 82, 8th line from top, for Janns read James.

Page 85, for 962-1274, read 960-1274.

INDEX

Of the Heads of Families bearing the name of Thacher.

www.ingramcontent.com/pod-product-compliance
Lightning Source LLC
Chambersburg PA
CBHW020032030726
47499CB00007B/2379